Demon Hunters 5: Cursed

Demon Hunters 5
Cursed

Avril Sabine

Cracked Acorn Productions
Australia

Demon Hunters 5: Cursed

Published by

Cracked Acorn Productions

PO Box 1365

Gympie, Queensland 4570

Australia

978-1-925131-94-9 (Kindle)

978-1-925617-41-2 (EPUB)

978-1-925131-95-6 (Print)

Genre: Young Adult Urban Fantasy/Horror

Copyright 2017 © Avril Sabine

Cover design by Caitlyn Petersen

*For my kids. Life would be extremely lacking
without each of you.*

After running into Luca, Penelope gets out of her car, worried he's hurt. When he tells her she's now his master and he's a genie, or a jinn as he says, she wants to put as much distance as possible between them. He's obviously insane. Others believe he's a genie, even though Penelope doesn't. They're willing to do anything to end her life so they can become Luca's master, including summoning demons.

*

This story was written by an Australian author using Australian spelling.

Chapter One

Penelope threaded her way through the crowd, a glass in one hand, her phone in the other as she checked the time. It was after eleven. Surely now she could go home. If only she could find one of her friends to let them know she was leaving. Dana had sworn this was the party she had to be at this weekend. That everyone who was anyone would be there. She'd driven nearly an hour and had wanted to leave not long after she'd arrived. She supposed it hadn't helped that within minutes of meeting up at the front door Dana, Suzie and Harrison had all wandered off in different directions, leaving her alone. She hadn't seen them since. Tucking her phone back in her purse, she took another sip of her drink.

She looked around the room again. No one. She was getting sick of this. If she didn't find them in the next ten minutes she was going home. They'd all come in their own vehicles so it wasn't like they needed her to stick around and give them a lift. Someone bumped into her, spilling their wine over her hand and forearm, muttering sorry as they hurried away. She stared after them. Obviously she'd waited too long to leave.

Ditching her glass on a nearby side table, she headed for the bathroom where she washed her hand and arm. This wasn't the way she wanted to spend a Saturday night. Not that she had any idea how she wanted to spend it. Or even how to spend the rest of her life. She'd felt this way ever since she'd finished year twelve back in November. It was now early February and she had no clue what to do with her days. Her grandmother was adamant that she needed to attend university, her father agreed. Her mother wanted her to help with her many charities until she figured out what she was going to do with her life. Neither option interested her. She needed to figure something out soon. Her grandmother's lectures were driving her crazy. Who cared if her grandmother had planned her entire life by the time she was eighteen? She wasn't anything like her grandmother. She was a different person even if she'd been named after the woman.

Drying her arm, Penelope sighed. This had to be the most boring party she'd been to this year. She'd find a quiet spot and ring her friends. If they didn't answer then that was too bad. She was going home. Wandering through the house, she sidestepped around the many groups talking and laughing, drinks in their hands. Finding a closed door, she opened it, slipping inside and shutting the door as she switched on the light.

Two people, with arms wrapped around each other, turned to face her. She stared back at them, her expression going blank as her mind tried to grasp what she was seeing. For a second she nearly reached for a strand of her light brown hair, that had recently been streaked a golden blond, to twist it between her fingers. It had been Suzie who'd pointed out it was something she did when she was uncomfortable and Harrison had been there too, his arm wrapped around her waist, not Suzie's.

Harrison cleared his throat. "Ahh, Penelope, I–"

Suzie interrupted him. "This isn't what it seems."

Inside she felt a stabbing pain. One of her best friends with her boyfriend. This wasn't meant to happen. Not to her. "Don't worry about it." She waved breezily, as if brushing away the moment. "I probably should thank the two of you."

"You should?" Suzie looked confused.

"Yes. I've been trying to think of a polite way to end things for the past week. I didn't want there to be any dramas since we attend the same parties and our parents are friends." She forced her lips to curve into a smile as she met Harrison's gaze. "I guess you must have picked up on that."

"Ahh, well…" Harrison shifted from one foot to the other.

"Although I am disappointed you didn't give me the same courtesy of finding a polite way of ending things first."

The door was flung open and Dana burst in speaking as she did. "Suzie, I lost sight of-" Her mouth dropped open as her gaze landed on Penelope. There were several seconds of drawn out silence before she spoke. "Pen."

The pain Penelope felt intensified. It took all her self-control to keep a smile in place. Both of her best friends had been lying to her. "This is good timing. Now I don't have to ring any of you and let you know I'm leaving."

"Already?" Dana asked. "It's too early to go home. The night has barely begun."

"I know, but I've had a better offer." Before they could ask her what offer, she strode from the room, letting her smile fade. The pain remained. She doubted it would fade so easily. The scene that had greeted her when she'd turned on the bedroom light played over in her mind in an endless loop.

She had no idea how she managed to walk through the house, find her convertible and get in the car without falling apart. The pain was nearly overwhelming. As bad as the one she'd experienced last month when she'd returned home to find the dog she'd rescued had been taken to the RSPCA. Her mother had been horrified that she'd considered keeping him and had offered to buy her a more suitable breed. She hadn't wanted a different one. She'd wanted hers. But it had been too late. Arriving at the RSPCA she'd learned he'd already been adopted and they'd refused to give her any details.

Seeing someone heading towards her, she started the car, checking in the rear view mirror before reversing. Catching a glimpse of her blue eyes she stared for a moment, surprised at how wide they were. They ached with unshed tears. She couldn't stay here. Not without ending up sitting here crying and being found by Dana, Suzie or Harrison. She wasn't going to give them the satisfaction of learning how much they'd hurt her. As she'd pointed out, they attended the same parties and their parents were friends and dragged them along to some of the same functions. She didn't want any of them looking at her with pity in their eyes or spreading rumours about her behind her back.

She reversed onto the road and headed towards home. Halfway there, she changed her mind, not wanting to risk them learning she'd been running home to hide. She drove aimlessly around Brisbane, not knowing where to go. She didn't feel sociable. All she wanted to do was go home and lock herself in her bedroom and try and forget every second of this night.

Ahead the streetlights changed to red and she slowed, watching a man stumble along the footpath ahead of her, cradling a bundled up blanket in his arms and wearing a black suit. She guessed he was drunk with how he couldn't manage a straight line. But surely he wouldn't be wandering around drunk at nearly midnight, carrying a baby. She couldn't imagine what else would be in the bundle. Not with how he held it.

The light changed and she drove forward, glancing at the man again. She was nearly past him when he stumbled and staggered in front of her car. She slammed on the brakes, swearing as she hit him, a sick feeling filling her stomach as the man disappeared from sight. Her first thought was of the bundle. The sick feeling increased and she fumbled with her seat belt, trying to unbuckle it. A glance at the time on her dash showed it wasn't yet midnight. In less than an hour her life had fallen apart. He had to be unharmed. Or at least not seriously hurt. Him and the bundle. She hadn't been going that fast.

The seat belt finally released and retracted. She turned on the hazard lights before getting out of the car. Her legs felt shaky and she stumbled in her high heels, something she hadn't done since she was a preteen. Not even when she was tipsy.

Before she could reach the man, he staggered to his feet, the wrapped bundle cradled against his chest as he weaved his way towards the footpath.

"Are you okay?" She almost groaned. "Of course you're not. I hit you. Where are you hurt?" Hurrying after him, she reached out to take hold of his arm and help him back to the footpath. He was all in black, including the shirt he wore under his suit jacket.

He pulled away before her fingers could make contact. "Don't touch me." There was a faint hint of an accent to his words.

"I'm sorry." She had no idea what to do.

He staggered with a growled curse, dragging himself upright before his knees hit the bitumen.

Penelope grabbed him by the wrist worried he'd collapse. She gasped when some of her fingers made contact with his skin. A sensation like pins and needles combined with static electricity shot through her hand.

He pulled roughly away from her. "I asked you not to touch me. Why did you not listen?"

She stared at him, massaging the fingers that had come in contact with him. "I was trying to help." She frowned. He didn't seem drunk. She began to wonder why he'd been walking like someone who'd downed an entire bottle of scotch. Was he sick?

He held the bundle out to her.

It was Penelope's turn to take a step backwards. She eyed the man warily. He was only slightly taller than her at five foot seven, his hair a dark blond, his eyes a piercing blue. It was his expression that made her wary. It was one of resignation, hate and arrogance. A strange combination. She glanced at the bundle. "Why would I want that?"

"It now belongs to you." He shoved it into her hands and she was forced to take it or let it drop.

The light blanket unwrapped enough that she could feel something within the folds. She moved them apart until she was staring at a man's gold watch, relieved it wasn't a baby like she'd first thought. Her gaze returned to the man, a question in it.

"Tell me to put the watch on you so I can touch it without pain."

Penelope made a sound that could have been any single syllable answer. The man took it for yes and slipped the watch onto her wrist so it hung loose like a bracelet. She pulled back from him, the blanket falling to the bitumen. "Who are you?" Her words, which she'd meant to be a demand, came out as a whisper.

"Conte Luca Martino Simoneti. Who are you?"

An Italian count? Impossible. Maybe he'd hit his head. Although there didn't seem to be any blood or bruises. She automatically answered him. "Penelope Elizabeth Grayson." She slowly shook her head, trying to make sense of the situation. "Can I help you? Give you a lift somewhere? To a hospital maybe?"

A bitter laugh escaped Luca. "I have no desire to go to a hospital. Not that it matters anyway. The question is, what can I help you with? How may I serve you, Master?"

Penelope took an uncertain step away from him and closer to the driver's door. "Ahh... I'm right thanks. Maybe you should go home. Get some sleep or something."

"Then let us go home, wherever that may now be."

Penelope swallowed loudly. Her heart started to race and she tried to judge the distance between her and the car door. It looked further away from her than Luca was. Could she make it in time?

The sound of running footsteps caused her to spin and face two people coming towards her. Was this all part of a hoax? Were these his accomplices? She took another step towards the open car door as she glanced between Luca and the two who ran towards her. They looked to be around her age. The girl had hazel eyes and dark honey coloured hair while the boy had dark hair and brown eyes. They both wore black jeans, black t-shirts and carried bows. Who carried bows around with them? A gun would have made more sense. If anything about this night could make sense.

They came to a stop, the girl looking from one to the other. Her gaze remained on Luca. "You're not a demon. I was expecting a demon."

"Who are you?" Penelope took another cautious step towards the driver's seat.

It was the young man who answered. "I'm Dan, this is Emily." He gestured towards the young woman beside him as he looked between Luca and Penelope followed by a glance at the mark around his wrist. It was a thin black line that went completely around it. "Why can't we sense demons?"

Luca looked from Dan to Emily. "You are hunters? What brought you here? There are no demons involved in this situation. I am a jinn."

"There must be," Emily said. "I wouldn't have had a premonition about this location and hour if there were no demons involved."

"What the hell is going on here?" Penelope felt the car door against her back as she took another step. She was nearly there. A few more steps and she could drive away and forget all about this night. Forget every single part of it. Starting with Harrison and Suzie. "Who are you people?"

"My master had a heart attack and was clinically dead for a few minutes. I had the chance of freedom, but you had to touch me." Luca glanced at Penelope before returning his attention to the hunters.

"You're not making sense." Penelope stepped sideways. Only another step and she'd be past the door. If she kept them talking she should be able to make it before any of them made a move towards her.

"I am a jinn. You are my master. I'm making perfect sense."

Penelope stared at Luca, forgetting to take another step. He'd said that before. "A what?"

"You'd probably know the term 'genie' better," Emily said.

Penelope laughed nervously. "Yeah, right. Sure. Where's your lamp?"

"You wear it." Luca gestured towards the watch at her wrist.

"So I rub the watch when I want three wishes? How modern of you." She shook her head. "I'm not an idiot. What is really going on here?" She should have gone straight home. First the party. Now this.

Emily held out a business card. "Call Father Joe when demons become involved. Leave your number with him and tell him you want me to call you."

When the girl continued to hold out the card, Penelope took it and tossed it into the car. "Sure." She was getting out of here and forgetting this day had ever happened. She retreated further. Although it was probably after midnight so she could forget about Sunday too.

"I know you don't believe us-"

Penelope interrupted Dan. "You're right. I have no idea what the three of you are planning, but I'm not staying to find out." Before she had a chance to get in her convertible, there was the sound of vehicles racing towards them and Luca threw himself at her, pushing her to the ground. He turned at the last second so she landed on top of him. The glass of the window rained over her and she tried to pull away from him. His arms tightened around her.

"Who wants to kill you?" Emily demanded from beside them on the ground.

Chapter Two

Penelope stared at the two people pressed against the bitumen. She opened her mouth but no words came out. She swallowed hard and tried again. "No one. Why would anyone want to kill me?"

"They want to kill her to regain control of me." Luca pushed her away from him and rose to a crouch. His hand held her effortlessly down when she tried to rise. "How can I protect you if you are going to stand up and let them know where you are?"

"If it's because of you, then why don't you go over there and deal with them?" Penelope glared up at Luca.

He gave an abrupt nod. "If that is what you desire, Exalted One. I am yours to command." He started to move away.

"Don't kill them," Emily said.

Luca looked over his shoulder. "I am not yours to command."

Emily turned to Penelope. "Tell him not to kill them. Their deaths will be on your soul, as if they were caused by you."

The words caused a shiver to go through Penelope. "Of course I don't want him to kill anyone." She shook her head. Could the night become any more bizarre? There was no way she was going to spend it plastered against the road. She turned to tell Luca, but he was gone. "Where did he go?" Had he heard what she'd said before he left? She didn't want anyone to die.

"He's knocked out the shooter." Dan peered over the rear of the car. "He can move fast." Dan winced. "That must have hurt." He paused. "He's still moving. The bullet barely slowed him down."

"Jinni are not much better than demons. They're made from the smokeless flame of a fire and can be as tricky as demons when following what you ask of them," Emily said.

Penelope opened her mouth to tell them they could quit with the theatrics. She closed it. It didn't matter. She had other plans. And they didn't include these people. It was all very well being unique, but there was such a thing as taking it too far. These people were bordering on the insane. She eased towards the open car door.

"What are you doing?" Emily grabbed hold of her arm.

Penelope shrugged the hand off. "I'm out of here."

"But-" Emily started to speak.

Dan interrupted her. "Don't forget free will. Everyone is allowed to choose how stupid they want to be. Isn't that what you told me?"

Emily shook her head. "Not exactly what I tried to teach you." Her lips curved up slightly.

"I'm not being stupid." Penelope glared at them. Who did they think they were?

"Come on, Em. We need to make a run for cover before she drives away. We've done all we can." Dan turned towards Penelope. "If you want help with your problems, call us. I haven't been dealing with demons for long, but Em has."

Emily nodded. "It's wrong to keep a jinn bound to you. Call us and we'll help you set him free."

Before Penelope could argue, Dan and Emily were dashing across the road towards a four-wheel-drive. She stared after them for a moment before she got in the car, turned off the hazard lights, started the engine and drove away. She was going home. And she was going to forget all about Luca, Emily and

Dan. The lot of them were delusional. Luca thinking he was an Italian noble and the other two who were… her mind couldn't think of a good enough description so she settled on odd.

It didn't matter who they were or what they thought they were doing. She'd managed to get away and wouldn't have to see them ever again. She started to relax a little. No one would believe what a bizarre night she'd experienced. If she told any of her friends they'd think she was on drugs.

Pain arrowed through her. For a few seconds she'd forgotten about Suzie and Harrison cheating on her. And Dana covering for them. She wasn't going to think of them either. An image of Luca's face returned to her mind. The angular cheekbones she would have killed for, a square jaw, thick hair, lightly tanned skin… she wasn't going to think about anyone. Not the certifiably insane and not the backstabbing ones she'd thought were friends.

Arriving home, she parked in the garage. She sat in the car for a moment, trying to make sense of everything. It was useless. Why had Suzie and Harrison gone behind her back? Why not break up with her? She started to get out of the car, but remembered the business card. Not wanting her parents to see it and worry about why she'd want to get in touch with a priest, she slipped it into her handbag to throw out later. It was going to be bad enough telling them about the broken window of her car.

After setting the house alarm, she headed to her room. The house was silent. Several dimmed lights had been left on. Reaching her bedroom, she kicked the door closed behind her and shed her clothes as she walked towards the ensuite. This night had been the worst one ever. She momentarily thought of her dog. She hadn't had the chance to name him. She'd narrowed it down to eight names, with Rusty and Teddy being her favourites. This year wasn't looking good. Twisting her hair up, she tucked the end into a bun to keep her hair atop her head and out of the way before pushing the ensuite door until she heard the soft click of it closing.

Stepping into the shower, she turned on the water, washing away the grime from the road. A pity she couldn't wash away the memories as easily. She had no idea what she was going to do about Suzie and Harrison. How was she going to face them?

She glanced at the watch, wondering if it was waterproof. Deciding it didn't matter since she had no plans to keep it, she finished showering.

Turning off the water, she stepped out of the

shower, fighting back the tears that threatened to fall. Harrison wasn't worth tears. None of them were. She grabbed a thick towel off the rail and dried herself, trying to empty her mind. Images kept forming. Luca, Harrison and Suzie, her dog, Dana, Emily and Dan. Wrapping the towel around herself, she opened the door to her bedroom, freezing when she saw Luca sitting in the armchair in the corner of her room. He looked out of place in the stark white and ivory room.

She clutched the towel to her chest. "What are you doing in here? How did you get in?" She'd set the alarm. A moment of doubt surfaced. No, she had set the alarm.

Luca rose gracefully to his feet, his lips curving into a smile that was tinged with bitterness. "Surely you've not forgotten so soon, Master."

He was going to keep up that charade? "Don't you get it? You're not welcome in my life. I don't know you, I don't want to know you, and you had no right to track me down like this. How did you find me?"

"I could find you anywhere. We're bound. You're my master until you die and I must protect you from all who would harm you unless you order me to put another's life above yours."

She thought of the moment he'd pushed her

towards the ground, glass showering over her. "You're not a genie."

"Jinn."

"Genie, jinn. It doesn't matter because you're not one. Now leave me alone."

Luca nodded curtly. "As you wish, Master. I'll give you enough space that you'll feel like you're alone." He stepped out of her room, closing the door behind him.

Continuing to clutch her towel, she opened the door and checked the hallway. "What are you doing out here? I thought you were going."

"How can I protect you if I leave?"

"You can't stay out here." Her parents would see him and she had no way to explain what he was doing here. Not that she knew if they were home.

Luca stood in front of her. "You'll have to step out of the way if you want me to return to your bedroom."

"What I want is for you to leave and not come back."

"That is one command I cannot follow. Not for any length of time."

Hearing a sound, she stepped out of the doorway. "Get back in my room." She had no idea how she'd explain Luca to her parents. Once he was in her room she shut the door and stared at him, trying to figure out why her first instinct had been to hide him. She should have been yelling for help.

He watched her, his face expressionless.

"How did you get in here without setting off the alarm?"

"It's one of my talents."

She started to ask him another question when she heard footsteps. "Ensuite. Now." Her mouth gaped at how quickly he crossed the room. A knock on her door had her closing her mouth with an audible sound and crossing the short distance to open it. Surely Luca hadn't moved that fast. Opening the door, she stared at her mother who wore a black dress and diamond bracelet with her perfect makeup.

"You have a visitor?"

Penelope shook her head.

"Your grandmother will be here late in the morning."

When she'd turned eighteen, her mother had gone from telling her not to have unsuitable people visiting, when her grandmother was due, to making subtle comments. She wasn't sure which she preferred. "Okay."

"Did you recently arrive home?"

"Yes. You too?" She nodded towards the clothes

her mother wore, trying to figure out why the moment felt surreal. There'd been numerous times they'd spoken like this.

"We went to the theatre. Your father took clients."

"Okay." She had no idea what to say, all she could think of was Luca in her ensuite.

"I'll see you in the morning. Your grandmother is expecting you to join us for lunch."

"Okay." The word felt awkward and repetitious, but no less awkward than the moment felt. She watched her mother walk away, her jewellery glinting as it caught the dim light, her blond hair piled artistically atop her head. It reminded her that her own was bundled up messily and she untwisted it to let it fall around her shoulders. Closing the door, she leaned back against it trying to figure out what to do. She couldn't stand here all night. Crossing to her walk-in wardrobe, she turned on the light before she closed the door, dressing in a pair of old jeans and a t-shirt. There was no way she was going to wear the black silky scrap of material that she called a nightie. Not while Luca was here.

Having no idea what else to do, she strode to her ensuite and flung open the door. Again her mouth dropped open.

Luca turned at her entrance, his shirt and jacket

hung over the towel rail, the tap running, blood smeared across his torso and dripping from two wounds. "Was there something else you wanted, Master?"

She clutched the door frame. "You need a doctor."

"I'll heal soon enough." He returned to cleaning the blood from his body, pressing a wad of tissues against one of the wounds that continued to drip.

"You'll die."

He met her gaze in the reflection of the mirror, his lips twisting into a bitter smile. "Not permanently. The curse will not allow it."

She leaned against the door frame, closing her eyes. Why was this happening to her?

"Are you well?"

Her eyes opened, at how close his voice sounded, to find he was in front of her. Before she could tell him to step away, his wounds caught her attention. Or more accurately his lack of wounds. "What happened?"

"You'll need to be more specific if you wish me to answer your question."

She started to reach out and touch his flesh where one of the wounds had been, stopping at the last second at the sight of blood. "They're gone."

"They healed once they were cleaned."

"This isn't possible." She closed her eyes again. "Go away, Luca."

Luca sighed lightly. "I really wish you'd make up your mind. One minute you send me away, the next you are telling me to come in and now you wish me gone again."

She opened her eyes to stare at him. "Are you mocking me?"

Luca did an odd bow that made Penelope frown. "I would never mock you, Exalted One. Your every wish is my command. I live only to serve you."

"Stop it. I've had enough of this. You're not a genie."

"Jinn."

Penelope waved his comment away. "Whatever. You aren't one. I don't know how you managed to track me down-" She stopped to stare at the watch she wore. "A tracking device." She pulled off the watch and shoved it at him. "Take it. I don't want it."

Luca put the watch on his wrist. "I'll carry it for you, but it'll not break the bonds between us. We're tied together until your death."

Chapter Three

Panic raced through Penelope at Luca's words. Did he plan to kill her? "I don't want you here. If you don't go I'll call the police. There are laws against stalking people." She tried to ignore his bare chest and the wounds that shouldn't be healed.

"You are tired. We'll talk in the morning after you have rested."

"Don't tell me what I am. I'm not tired." As if she didn't have enough people in her life telling her how she felt and what she should be doing.

"Would you rather I said you were afraid and bordering on hysteria?"

"I'm not." She glared at him, trying to keep the fear from her voice.

"How can I serve you if I do not know how you feel?"

Shaking her head, she backed away. "Please." She wasn't sure what she was asking.

"You're the first of my masters who hasn't immediately demanded I do something for you. Why?"

She stopped her slow retreat. "Ask you to do something?"

"You're my master. I must serve you. Why haven't you asked something of me?"

"I don't believe you're a genie."

"Jinn."

"They don't exist."

"Then why not set me a task?"

"A task?"

"Yes. Do you want someone killed? An item fetched? Are you looking for revenge?"

She took a step towards him, her hand rising. "Don't kill anyone."

"Your wish is my command. I'll not take a life except to save yours."

"Not even then." She shook her head. "People don't offer to kill. It's wrong."

"Not that I have noticed." He sounded weary.

"How old are you, Luca?"

"Forever nineteen."

"When did you turn nineteen?"

"1290."

The date rang in her mind like an echo. "I should be terrified of you. I should run screaming."

"It's the bond. You know I cannot harm you."

She shook her head. "I don't know that. Not at all. You're crazy. Completely and utterly crazy." Yet he didn't seem crazy. His tone of voice, the way he held himself and the look in his eyes all made him appear sane. "Why me?"

"Because you touched me. Why did you touch me?"

"I thought you were about to collapse. Why were you stumbling about like a drunk?"

"I was fighting to keep hold of the watch. No jinn can touch that which they are bound to unless their master gives them permission."

"I can't–" She broke off, taking a step away. "No more. Not tonight." She stared at him a moment. "I'm tired."

Luca stepped back and gestured towards her bed. "Sleep. I'll keep you safe. No harm will come to you while I watch over you."

She wanted to protest that she didn't need anyone to keep her safe. Exhaustion dragged at her and tears threatened to fall. If he was meant to keep her from harm, he was too late. Harrison had already hurt her.

Luca rushed forward, his hands wrapping around her upper arms. "What is wrong? How can I alleviate your pain?"

She slowly shook her head, not wanting to talk about it.

"Deny it all you wish, but I can feel your pain through our bond."

The strength and warmth of his hands dragged her away from her memories. "You can read my mind?"

"No. Feel strong emotions."

"Can I do the same?"

"If you concentrate."

She focused on him, sensing nothing different. "You're lying."

He grinned momentarily. "You think I would let my emotions betray me? I've had centuries of keeping them under control."

She felt the barest hint of an emotion, pretty sure it wasn't hers. "Pride."

He inclined his head. "Very good."

Her emotions were so tangled she couldn't sort them out. Why had she stopped to help him? But what else could she have done? She'd run into him.

"Sleep. Things will be clearer in the morning." Letting go of her, he stepped away. "I've never lost a master to misfortune. They all died of old age."

Again she felt that hint of pride. "You don't seem the sort to want to be someone's slave. Why protect your masters?"

"I have no choice. I must protect them to the best of my ability. And you are wrong. A jinn is less than a slave. They have more freedom than I do. I must follow your every command. I don't have the choice of refusal."

"Slaves wouldn't be able to refuse."

"They could refuse. It'd lead to punishment, but they could disobey an order. I'm compelled to obey."

She felt a tinge of sorrow and wanted to comfort him. It took her a moment to realise it wasn't her sorrow. The reality of the situation rushed through her and she stumbled to her bed, sitting down hard. This couldn't be happening. It was impossible.

Luca came forward to kneel at her feet so he could look up at her. "What do you wish me to do?"

"This is real." Her words were whisper soft.

Luca inclined his head.

"What am I meant to do?"

"I am yours to do with as you wish. Until your death many decades from now."

She clasped her hands together to prevent them from twisting a lock of hair. "I don't know what to do with my own life. How am I meant to know what to do with yours? I don't want this."

"Then you should not have touched me."

"I didn't know. I was trying to help."

"If you truly want to help, set me free. If you don't, I'll always be bound to you. Always at your beck and call. Unable to leave, unable to be taken from you."

"Mine?"

"Yes."

She thought of Harrison and the dog that had been taken away. "Always?"

"What are you thinking?"

So many things had been taken from her. "I have a tendency to be drawn to unsuitable things. People, items, dogs." Or at least that's what she was regularly told by her grandmother and mother. "What if my parents send you away?"

"I'll find a way to stay with you that doesn't cause problems for you."

She stared into his piercing blue eyes.

"What are you thinking?"

"I can't."

"You can't do what?"

"Let you go."

He rose, stepping back from her. "None of you can." His voice was flat, his face expressionless.

"I'm sorry." How could she let go of the one person who couldn't be taken from her? It was a strange feeling knowing he couldn't leave, couldn't be stolen from her and would always be hers. It took her a moment to realise what the feeling was. Reassuring. It was comforting and reassuring.

"What made you make that decision?"

She almost didn't answer him, but he deserved some kind of reply. "Life."

He inclined his head, taking several steps away from her.

Her gaze was drawn to his bare chest. "You need more clothes."

"I'll acquire them while you sleep if you promise not to leave the house without me to protect you."

She wanted to argue his words, but had the feeling he wouldn't accept anything other than her promise. "Okay."

He held her gaze for a moment. "If you break your promise I will not trust your words in the future and will always remain at your side to protect you."

"I could send you away."

"Of a fashion."

She was too tired for this conversation. "I'll wait here until you return."

He examined her for a moment, his gaze mostly

focused on her face. With another nod, he returned to the bathroom, leaving the door open.

She watched him clean off the last of the blood and dress before letting himself out of her room, closing the door softly behind him. She stared at the painted, timber door. Her mind was a jumble and her emotions tangled. How had life become so strange? And complicated. It was a few minutes before she could bring herself to move and finish getting ready for bed.

Sleep was dreamless and she woke to find Luca sitting in the armchair, watching her. "Do you have to do that?"

"Do what exactly?"

"Watch me."

"Watching over you."

"You were watching me." Annoyance arrowed through her and she tossed back the bed sheets. "I don't want you to do that. It's creepy." She wanted to ask if she snored. Or drooled in her sleep. Pressing her lips together, she continued to glare at him. "How would you like someone staring at you while you slept?"

"I don't need to keep my gaze on you to be able to watch over you while you sleep."

"Then watch over me from somewhere else."

"Where else am I meant to remain? You wouldn't let me wait in the hallway."

She couldn't deal with this right now. She was barely awake, needed a shower and something to eat. "I thought you were getting other clothes. Why are you wearing your suit?"

"These are other clothes."

"You got more suits?"

Luca inclined his head.

"You can't dress like that. You look like the morning after."

"The morning after what?"

"The morning after unexpectedly spending the night with someone and still dressed in the same clothes from the evening before."

"Ah. You're concerned what your parents will think."

More what her grandmother would think, but he was close enough. "Yes. You need casual clothes. Ones a teenager would wear on the weekend."

"You'll remain here while I locate clothes you will find appropriate."

She was tempted to argue. Wasn't she meant to be the master? It sounded like he was the one throwing orders around. "My grandmother is coming here to have lunch with my parents and me."

He inclined his head. "I'll be as quick as possible." He headed for the bedroom door.

"You can't go out that way. Someone will see you."

"I'll make certain no one does." He listened at the door before he left the room.

Chapter Four

Penelope stared at the door Luca had closed behind him. She'd half expected to wake up this morning to find he'd been a figment of her imagination. Uncertain if she was happy about learning he was real, she got ready for the day. She was tempted to wear a pair of jeans, but didn't feel up to a lecture from her grandmother. She chose a summer dress, one that would hopefully meet her approval. Sometimes she didn't know why she bothered as very little met her grandmother's approval.

Leaving her room, she headed towards the kitchen, running into her father before she reached it. "Morning."

"What happened to your car window?"

She'd forgotten about it. "Someone threw a rock." For a moment she was tempted to tell him it had been shot so she could see his reaction.

"I'll arrange for a replacement."

"Okay."

"Did your mother inform you your grandmother will join us for lunch?"

"Yes."

"I will see you then."

She turned to watch him walk away, sighing. Maybe she shouldn't have bothered telling Luca to wear casual clothes. Her father obviously didn't know that weekends weren't for suits. More than likely he'd stay long enough to join them for lunch before working the rest of the day. It wasn't like he didn't have the option of working less hours. She'd come to the conclusion, years ago, that he preferred to work long hours. Either that or it was the perfect excuse not to spend time with her.

Her stomach rumbled and she continued towards the kitchen. The housekeeper was bustling around preparing an elaborate lunch. One that was more than likely not going to be good enough for her grandmother.

She made herself a piece of toast, declining the housekeeper's offer to make her something more substantial, and wandered through the house eating it. She felt lost. Normally she'd have rung Dana by now and talked about the previous night's party as she ate. There was no one she could phone. Not that the party was worth talking about. It had been terrible from the start, becoming worse by the minute. A sharp pain arrowed through her as she tried not to think about Harrison and Suzie.

She was still wandering around aimlessly when her grandmother arrived, offering her a cheek for a kiss. "Morning, Grandmother." The woman eyed her up and down, her white-blond hair perfectly styled, her makeup and numerous plastic surgeries reducing the appearance of age and her outfit appropriate for a Sunday lunch. At least it was according to her grandmother. She braced herself for the cutting remark.

"If you are going to be out late at night at least use makeup the next morning to hide the effects of lack of sleep, Penelope."

There it was. Her looks rather than her clothes. Maybe she'd got her clothes right for a change. "I didn't realise it showed that much."

"I'll inform the staff that you need better lighting in your bathroom."

She managed a nod, when she would have preferred to point out that a single housekeeper wasn't exactly staff.

Her grandmother looked her up and down again.

"I will see that better lighting is also put in your dressing room."

And there it was. Her dress wasn't any good either. "Thank you." She pressed her lips together to prevent other words from escaping. It was a waste of time arguing with her grandmother.

"Where are your parents? Have they forgotten I was due to arrive for lunch?"

Penelope shook her head. As if they'd dare. "They both reminded me you were joining us." They were probably smart enough to remain out of sight until the last minute. "Not that I needed reminding."

"Well come and join me in the sitting room while we wait for lunch to be served. You can tell me what you have been doing lately."

A glance around showed there was no escape. "Okay."

"Speak up, Penelope. Mumbling is highly unattractive."

So were many things according to her grandmother. She nodded, following her grandmother to the sitting room, or what everyone else in the family called the lounge room. She thought of her phone she'd left in her room since there was no one she wanted to talk to or hear from. If she'd brought it with her she'd at least have some idea of how long she'd be stuck trying to answer the many questions her grandmother was sure to ask. Ones she had no idea how to answer. She didn't know what she wanted to do with her life. If she did, she'd already be doing it.

Time stretched out and Penelope regularly glanced towards the doorway in the hope she'd see one of her parents. Neither appeared and she was left to stumble through the awkward conversation of what she should be doing with her life and listen to how she was wasting her time. She nearly jumped to her feet when the housekeeper notified them lunch was ready. It took a great deal of self-control to maintain a suitable speed and a neutral expression. Luckily she'd had years of practice.

Lunch was accompanied by more of her grandmother's complaints and she was glad when the meal ended and she escaped with a mumbled excuse. Her grandmother's reminder not to mumble followed her from the room. Retreating to her bedroom, she stepped inside, closing the door and her eyes as she leaned back against it.

"Can I help?"

Opening her eyes, she nearly screamed to find Luca standing in front of her. She pressed her hand over her mouth, preventing the scream from escaping. Her other hand she pressed against her heart, willing it to slow.

"Is something wrong?"

She lowered her hand from her mouth, keeping the other one in place. "Don't sneak up on me."

"Silence is part of the curse."

She pressed her hand against his chest so that he stepped back from her. "You need to tell me everything." She looked him up and down, taking note of his black trousers and long sleeved shirt. "I don't think you know how to do casual, but I guess this outfit is better than a suit."

"My previous master preferred the more formal look. If you wish me to wear something in particular, you only have to say. Or if you prefer me to never wear suits, tell me that too."

"They have their place." And they certainly looked good on him. Although what he was wearing also looked good. Turning away from him she tried to think of something to say. Admiring Luca seemed wrong somehow. She had a feeling it was because she owned him. She shied away from that thought too. "You were going to tell me everything." Stepping around him she headed for her bed, which was still unmade, and sat on it.

He faced her. "I believe it was a case of you

ordering me to tell you everything. You'll have to be a little more specific. What in particular do you wish me to tell you?"

"Have you always been a genie?" She spoke again before he could. "Jinn."

"No. I was human once. I am not a true jinn. He didn't want me to have the full power of one. If he could, he would have given me only the curse."

"What happened? How did you become one?"

"Are you sure you want to know these details?"

She tried to read his expression, but it was impossible. There was also no hint of emotion from him. "You don't want to tell me, do you?"

"If you order me, I must obey."

She started to tell him it was okay. That she didn't need to know. But what was he hiding? What if it was important? "Tell me who you were before you became a jinn and why you became one."

He stared at her for a moment before inclining his head and retreating to the armchair. "I was a younger son, two brothers ahead of me, so I went with a group of Italians to Acre for the last crusade. Obviously we didn't know it was the last one. It was 1290 and none of us had expected things to be the way they were. We drank to forget. It didn't help. Nothing did." He fell silent, his eyes becoming unfocused.

She was again tempted to say he didn't need to explain anything. He spoke before she could tell him she'd changed her mind.

"I didn't know why I was dragged before Tahir ibn Ishaq. I learned afterwards. I had been passed out drunk when my companions killed his daughter Marajil bint Tahir. I could not tell you what she looked like. But that didn't matter. I was in the same room, they were the ones I'd travelled to Acre with and the ones I fought beside. Her servant escaped and sought help. When the soldiers and shayateen arrived she was dead. They tried to capture my companions. All were killed. Except me."

"What are shayateen?"

"A shaitan is a jinn that likes to antagonise humans. Like the jinni they cannot open locks or untie knots."

"Didn't you call them a shayateen?"

Luca smiled. "One is plural, the other singular. Shaitan and jinn are singular. Shayateen and jinni are plural." His smile faded. "I learned far more of Tahir's language than I ever wished to know. He could not become my master, the curse doesn't work that way, but he made sure there was someone there to take that position. A man known for his cruelty."

She didn't know what to ask him next. About his first master, how he was made or more about the jinni. "I thought you said jinni can't open locks. How did you get inside?"

"When Tahir had the shayateen turn me into a jinn, with the help of a smokeless fire, they locked me in my earthly form. This means I don't have the full power of the jinni. I can't grant wishes, possess a human, become invisible, fly or take on the form of an animal. But I can open locks even though it feels like I'm being passed through the smokeless flame again, the heat burning away my ties to the human world."

"What can you do?"

"The question they all ask." There was a bitterness to his voice. "I can see further, hear better, smell the faintest of scents and move faster than a human. I cannot die even though I can be killed time and time again. As long as my body isn't burned to ash I'll rise again and heal to the original state I was in when I was cursed. I have a greater than average chance of persuading people in the service of my master, can blend with the shadows and walk silently."

"Have you ever used your persuading ability on me?"

"None of my abilities can be used against you, only in your service, Exalted One."

"Don't call me that." It made her feel uncomfortable.

Luca inclined his head.

"You said the curse can be broken."

He took off the watch and came forward, showing her the back of it. "If I hadn't had a medallion, one would have been created for me. This is half of my family's seal, a medallion my family gave me to wear when I left for the crusades. My last master had it turned into the back of the watch so he could always keep it with him. The previous one wore it as a medallion."

She stared at the back of the watch, the image of a comet on part of it. "The medallion's broken?"

Luca nodded. "It was broken when I was made a jinn. The family coat of arms is a comet and a tower. When they're rejoined the curse will be broken and I can live out the rest of my natural life as a human. Either that or I must be without a master for one turn of the moon. For that to happen, my master must first die."

"I'm not going to die."

"None of my masters ever want to die." He remained silent a moment. "Or set me free."

His words made her feel uncomfortable. "I can't."

"You can. You choose not to."

Rising to her feet, she stepped forward so he had to take a step back. "I need to go out. I can't sit around here all day."

"Where are we going?"

"I don't know where you're going, but I'm going out." It didn't matter where. Anything had to be better than sitting around thinking about ex-friends and the uncomfortable feelings keeping Luca caused. Oddly enough they didn't prevent the reassuring feeling from remaining.

"Where you go, so do I."

Chapter Five

A shiver went through Penelope at Luca's words. She was tempted to ask him if that was a threat or a promise. She decided she didn't want to know. Or she did, but she was afraid to learn the answer. Stepping past him, she headed for her walk-in wardrobe, stopping in the doorway to turn and look at him. He was facing her. "If you're going with me we might as well go shopping for some clothes for you. Something more casual than what you're wearing." Certain she felt a fleeting hint of annoyance come from him, she grinned. "You definitely need jeans." Her gaze was drawn to his legs before she retreated to her walk-in wardrobe. Turning on the light she shut the door.

Leaning against the door, she closed her eyes, trying not to picture Luca in jeans. Maybe she should get him something ugly to wear. He was far too good looking as it was. Taking a deep breath she opened her eyes and pushed away from the door. She couldn't hide in here all afternoon.

Once she was dressed, Penelope grabbed her phone and purse from the handbag she'd used last night and put them in one that suited jeans. Reaching the car, she sighed when she remembered the broken window. For a moment she was tempted to return to her room and change out of her jeans. She'd expected to be in air conditioning, not subjected to the heat of summer.

"Is something wrong?"

Shaking her head, she got in the car and started it once Luca was in the passenger seat.

"You say that a lot."

"What do you mean?"

"That nothing is wrong when it clearly is."

"Then why ask me if something is wrong. Why not tell me?" She reversed out of the garage and headed towards the city.

"Politeness. It'll take time to become accustomed to the fact you don't have a gun and aren't likely to use it when you're annoyed with me."

"He–" She broke off, not wanting to risk learning the details. She thought of a question that seemed safer. "How many times have you died?"

"I lost count before the first century ended."

The matter of fact tone of his voice made pain arrow through her and she had to pull over, glad the traffic was light. "Luca-"

He captured her hand before she could touch him. "You asked the question. Why ask if you don't want to know the answer?"

"I didn't expect that answer."

"What did you expect?"

"A number." Her gaze was drawn to his hand that continued to hold hers. "One you could count on a single hand. Two at the most."

"That amount would cover the first year."

Her gaze travelled upwards until she met his piercing blue eyes. "Aren't you angry?"

"Resigned. I've had a lot of time to become accustomed to it."

"You look so young I sometimes forget how old you are. Do you feel centuries old?"

He didn't answer immediately. "I feel both young and old."

"That doesn't make sense."

"I feel nineteen even though logically I've lived for centuries and have experienced far more than any nineteen-year-old could ever have experienced. I'm frozen in time, Penelope."

"Pen. My friends call me Pen."

"I am not your friend. Penelope. You're my master and I'm compelled to do everything you order of me."

"So I could order you to call me Pen and you would."

"Yes."

Her lips parted, but that was as far as she got. She couldn't bring herself to order him to call her by her nickname.

"Is it an order?"

She shook her head. This was becoming worse by the second. What had she been thinking wanting to keep him? "You can choose what you want to do, even ignore what I ask of you."

"Regarding everything?"

There was something about his tone of voice that made her hesitate. "Unless I specifically tell you it's an order." She felt a hint of confusion and it took her a second to realise it wasn't hers.

"Why would you make that offer?"

She couldn't meet his gaze any longer. "I'm sorry."

"What are you sorry about?"

"This is wrong. I-" The words stuck in her throat and she was unable to speak them, pain arrowing through her as she thought of Harrison and the dog. She couldn't bring herself to set him free.

He let go of her hand. "You do not make sense."

"I know." Silence fell in the car and she eventually looked at Luca to find him staring at her. "Ask my grandmother. She'll assure you I'm always drawn to inappropriate things and I constantly make senseless choices."

"I wouldn't listen to anything she has to say. She's far too bitter and dissatisfied that she's incapable of seeing the good."

She smiled. "I can't disagree with that comment. But I was named for her so she feels an obligation to guide me." Her smile vanished. "Do you see the good? Or is it impossible after all these years?"

He didn't answer immediately. "There is good."

"But do you see it?"

"I'm not sure what you're asking."

She tried to figure out a way to explain it. "Do you experience it?"

"No."

Silence filled the car as she tried to think what to say. Warmth flowed in the broken window competing with the cold of the air conditioner.

"Are we going shopping or have you changed your mind?"

Shaking her head, she looked away from him, taking a deep breath as she tried to focus on the traffic. The rest of the drive was silent, but she couldn't stop thinking about his answer. Everything he said had her feeling more guilty than before. She had to let him go, but she had no idea how. Not the mechanics, but the actual letting go.

She parked the car then turned in her seat so she could face him. "What would you do if you were set free?"

"Go home."

"Home? You have a home?"

"The place I was born. I haven't seen it since the day I left in 1290. None of my masters have ever gone there."

"You have family?"

Luca smiled wryly. "Not exactly. They're related. My brothers' descendents. It isn't possible for me to tell them who I am."

"What does it look like?"

"If you lend me your phone I can show you."

She handed over her phone, taking it back after he pulled up a website. She stared at the castle, seeing that it held guided tours. Scrolling through the page, she saw a man who bore a strong resemblance to Luca. She looked from her phone to him.

"My oldest brother's descendent."

She looked at another page. Smiling as she read about the legend of the three brothers. "You hid your swords? Is that true?"

"Yes. I took my father's sword. We hid our swords to be collected when I returned from the crusades. I never returned so they were left hidden. A memorial of sorts."

"Could you find them?" She looked at him when he didn't answer.

"Of course."

She barely managed not to laugh at the hint of pride she felt, nearly gone before she registered it. Returning her phone to her handbag, she took out her keys. "Time to go shopping."

"You're not worried someone will steal your car since it can't be locked?"

She shrugged. "It's insured." Her father would be annoyed, but that was nothing new. "Come on. Let's get you some clothes."

They spent far longer shopping than Penelope had expected and by the time they headed towards the exit, Luca was laden down with bags. Not all of them for him. Her steps slowed as she passed a pet shop, coming to a halt when she saw the puppy in the final display. He looked up at her with soulful eyes, one brown, one milky white, a sign begging someone to adopt him and explaining an accident had taken part of his sight.

She knelt in front of him, her hand against the window, her heart aching to take him home. He came forward, pressing his nose against the glass and a wave of longing rushed over her.

"You want this animal?"

"No." She spoke the word quickly, worried she'd give in and say yes.

"Then why do I feel so much longing from you?"

She looked up at Luca. "It doesn't matter. He'd be taken from me."

"I wouldn't allow it."

She wanted to say yes. Wanted even more to ask him to find the dog she'd rescued. Forcing herself to her feet, she headed towards the car park, unable to speak.

Luca walked at her side. "What is wrong?"

She glanced at him. "Why ask when you know I'm not going to answer?" She sensed amusement from him.

"Maybe one day I'll be lucky."

"I had a dog."

"What was your dog named?'

"I didn't have him long enough to decide on a

name." Maybe she would have ended up choosing Rusty for his reddish brown coat. Although he'd had that worn look of a well loved teddy bear.

"He died?"

"No."

"He was stolen?"

"Not exactly."

"You do understand you can order me to find him for you."

"I guessed that."

"Why haven't you? I can feel your pain and longing when you think of him."

Reaching the car, she leaned back against it, staring at Luca a moment before she could speak. "Because I'd only lose him again. He isn't suitable."

"According to who?"

"My mother."

Luca put the shopping bags in the car. "Do you really not understand how all this works?"

She frowned. "What do you mean?"

"If you want wealth, I have to find a way to get it for you. If you want your own place, jewels, a dog, it is yours. You have but to order me to do your bidding and I'll be forced to find a way to carry it out."

"How would you make me wealthy?"

"The easiest is to steal it."

"No. That's wrong."

"There are other ways. Would you be interested in wealth if it could be acquired without stealing it?"

"No. I don't know." She shook her head, confusion making it impossible for her to know exactly how to answer him. She'd figure it out later. "We need to find a Laundromat so we can wash your new clothes. I can't exactly ask the housekeeper to wash them without my parents finding out."

"Do you want me to drive?"

"You can drive?"

"I might be centuries old, but I haven't remained living in the past. I've been driving far longer than you."

"You have a license?"

He nodded. "My identification was updated this year. It tends to need to be done every ten years or I'm accused of impersonation."

She shook her head. "I can drive." She slid behind the wheel of her car. How was she meant to sort out identification for him in ten years time? The thought made her pause. She couldn't keep him. It was wrong. But she couldn't convince herself to let him go. He was hers. No one could take him from her.

Chapter Six

Once Luca's clothes had been washed and dried, they returned home, taking the packages to Penelope's room. The bed was made and the clothes that had been left on the floor were now gone, the handbag hanging in her walk-in wardrobe where they put Luca's clothes. The ones she bought for herself went in the clothes basket in her ensuite.

Penelope stared at the clothes at the back of her walk-in wardrobe. "Our housekeeper is going to notice them."

"Tell her it isn't necessary for her to take care of your room. That you'll do it in future."

"I'm not about to clean my room." She wouldn't have a clue where to start.

"I'll take care of it."

"Oh."

"You think I am not capable?"

She shook her head. "No. I just didn't think of it." Things were becoming more complicated by the minute. She didn't want to think about it. "Let's go out for dinner."

Luca nodded.

"What's wrong?" She'd barely felt his emotion. It had been masked before she'd had a chance to figure it out.

"Are you ordering me to tell you?"

"Of course not."

"Then nothing is wrong."

She was tempted to tell him it was an order.

"You're annoyed."

"Yes."

"Is it an order?"

She shook her head. "You don't have to tell me."

"But you wish I would."

"Of course I do."

"I don't think I'll ever understand you."

Penelope laughed, more bitterness than amusement in the sound. "My mother regularly tells me that. Not in the confused way you did. In an insulting kind of way. Like there's something wrong with me."

He stepped close, his piercing blue eyes staring directly at her. "There is nothing wrong with you."

"You don't know me well enough to say that."

"You would be surprised what I do know about you."

Her lips parted, but she couldn't bring herself to ask. If it was bad, she didn't want to know. "Dinner?"

He didn't answer immediately, eventually inclining his head. "If that is what you desire."

She really wished he hadn't used that word. Dinner was the last thing she desired. She'd spent most of the afternoon fighting against that. She pushed away the feelings again.

Luca reached out to run his finger along her cheek. "I'm surprised you don't order me to be your lover."

"No. Never." She thought of Harrison and Suzie wrapped in each other's arms.

"Why never?"

"Is it wrong to be wanted for myself?" Her words were soft.

His were equally quiet. "Not at all." He paused a moment. "Why will you not set me free? If you don't need a jinn, why keep me?"

"I–" She closed her eyes, unable to meet his gaze. Sadness washed over her and she felt his hands on her shoulders.

"Is there a point in asking you what is wrong?"

She was alone. How much more wrong could you get than that? Not through choice. That would be different. Through dishonesty and treachery. She kept her eyes closed, not wanting to see his eyes. They saw too much and she feared what she might see reflected back in them. She was about to tell him he wouldn't understand, then realised he'd probably understand more than most.

"Penelope?"

She opened her eyes, meeting his gaze. The piercing blue reflected only her image. "Did you have any friends over the centuries?"

"It was strongly discouraged."

"How strongly?"

"Death."

"Whose death?'

"Mine and theirs."

She tried to swallow, fighting back the tears that wanted to fall. "I'm sorry."

"You truly are." There was wonder in his voice. "How can you be bothered by some things and yet not by others?"

She knew he meant being his master. "I'm more bothered by other things than you know." She pulled away from his hands. "We're going out to dinner." She forced her feelings away and her face to become expressionless.

"You're very good at that."

"At what?"

"Hiding your emotions. It makes me wonder how much practice you've had."

She met his gaze before turning away and gathering her handbag. "Far too much." Opening the bedroom door, she looked over her shoulder. "Are you coming?"

"I'll meet you at your vehicle."

She closed the door behind her, her steps slow as she wondered what he was up to. He joined her as she reached the car, a blur of movement until he came to a stop beside her. She pressed her hand against her heart. "You changed." He wore jeans and a t-shirt, both of them black. He'd insisted on the colour, initially not telling her why. She'd had to ask several times before he said blood was less noticeable against black. The answer had chilled her, more for the matter of fact tone of voice that had accompanied his words.

He took the car keys from her. "I'll drive. You're too distracted. I have never lost a master to misadventure and I'll not do so tonight."

She was tempted to argue, but he was right. She was distracted even though she'd managed to shut down her emotions. Sinking into the passenger seat, she closed her eyes, trying not to think of anything.

She had to let him go. Eventually. A week. She wanted one week where she didn't fear losing something or someone.

"Where do you wish to go?" Luca started the engine.

"I don't care."

They remained silent and Penelope kept her eyes closed until the car stopped and the engine was turned off. She smiled when she spotted a familiar restaurant. One she'd been to numerous times and was perfectly suited to their more casual attire. Her smile vanished when they entered and she saw Suzie and Harrison seated at a table.

Suzie spotted them and waved them over. "You should join us." She beckoned a waiter forward before Penelope could speak.

Panic rushed through her as she tried to keep her expression neutral and her hands away from her hair. "I really-"

"It's no trouble. We've barely ordered," Suzie said.

Luca interrupted, sliding his arm around Penelope's waist and drawing her close. "What you keep preventing Pen from telling you is that we're looking forward to dining alone." He smiled before turning his gaze on Penelope.

The look in his eyes had her sagging against his

side, struggling to remind herself it was an act. She returned his smile. "Exactly. Thank you." She placed her hand against his heart, almost surprised to feel it beat within his chest. "Suzie has a tendency to talk too fast and give no one a chance to say their piece."

"Where are you from?" Suzie demanded. "I can't place your accent and I'm really good with accents."

"I've travelled the majority of my life." Luca nodded at each of them. "If you will excuse us, we need to organise a table."

"You won't get one if you haven't booked," Suzie warned.

"You would be surprised at how persuasive I can be when I want something." Luca again smiled at Penelope.

Harrison half rose from his seat. "Pen, I–"

Suzie interrupted. "Call us, Pen. We'll have to organise a double date some time."

She returned Suzie's insincere smile with one of her own. "I'll let you know when I have some free time." She wanted to beg Luca to get her away from the table.

With another nod, Luca walked away, his arm remaining around Penelope's waist. "An ex lover?"

"Ex boyfriend and ex best friend."

"I'm sorry you had to suffer that. Next time try

experiencing a bit of anger and then I'll know better how to act."

She had no idea how to reply to his comment and was relieved when he turned away to arrange a table. Within minutes they were seated and their orders taken. "How did you manage that?"

"Persuasion."

"Oh." She remembered what he'd told her earlier. "Give me a week."

"A week for what exactly?"

She reached across the table to take his hand. "One week and then I'll set you free. Please."

"The choice is yours."

"Next Sunday I'll set you free."

"It isn't so simple. The other half of the medallion isn't in this world. We would have to travel to the home of the jinni to find it."

"Then we'll go there. After you give me a week."

"What will one week do for you?"

She didn't want to tell him. Didn't want to see pity in his eyes. But he deserved an answer. Her gaze dropped to the table before she was able to speak. "I want to know what it feels like not to lose something or someone. To know it's impossible to have you taken from me or for you to leave."

"Are you a virgin?"

"What?" His question had her raising her voice, lowering it after a glance at the nearby tables. "Why would you ask that?"

"Only a virgin, of the age of consent, can fit the two halves of the medallion back together in the resting place of Solomon. In Queensland that is sixteen."

"Oh."

His hand tightened on hers. "It was a nice offer. You'll have longer than your week. It will be you who is the one taken from me."

There was a strange note in his voice that she couldn't figure out. "Have you ever loved any of your masters?"

"Not a single one. No previous master has ever been worthy of such an emotion."

She couldn't bring herself to ask the question she really wanted to know. Was she? She momentarily glanced away. "Why couldn't Suzie place your accent? She was right when she said she's really good with accents. She has a thing for them."

"Accents of a country change over time. There are none alive who would have my accent. Even those from my time wouldn't recognise mine as I've managed to lose almost all trace of it."

"Oh."

Luca let go of her hand. "You're constantly made uncomfortable by my answers. It baffles me half the time. Why would that make you uncomfortable?"

"All you've lost."

"What about all I've gained?'

"A lifetime of servitude?"

"I've seen the rise and fall of nations."

"Is that enough?"

Again he was silent. "It's been a long time since I've had a conversation. Normally I'm only called upon to report details or seek out information."

"You aren't going to answer my question, are you?"

The meal arrived and they both fell silent until the waiter left. Luca met her gaze. "It isn't something I've dwelt upon. Nothing is ever all good or all bad."

They'd nearly finished eating when Penelope thought of a solution. "I could ring the hunters. They might know a virgin." She felt a moment of surprise from him before it was masked.

He stared at her. "You are serious about setting me free."

"Yes. After a week."

"Do I take it you know none that fit the requirements?'

She laughed. "Not likely."

"We'll call the hunters next Sunday." Luca finished his meal, rising to his feet and holding out his hand. "Where would you like to go next?"

Chapter Seven

It was a moment before Penelope could take Luca's hand and stand up. "I don't know." She didn't want to go home. "Anywhere."

Luca paid for the meal before they left, returning the wallet to his pocket as they walked outside.

"Where did you get the money from?"

"Left over from my previous master."

"You shouldn't spend it on me. You'll need it when you're free."

"I have treasure hidden all around the world in the hope that one day I'll be free. Spoils of war, valuables taken from my masters, some hidden on their behalf and never collected by them and ones I saw others hide. I have more wealth than I could possibly use in one mortal lifetime."

"Oh."

Luca glanced at her before he opened the passenger

door of the car, holding it open for her. "How can that make you feel uncomfortable?"

"Not uncomfortable exactly. Kind of sad and wishing I didn't make you think of the centuries you'd hoped to be set free only to remain a jinn."

He continued to hold the car door, his gaze upon her. "You are very strange."

"Why? Because I feel compassion?"

"No. Because you don't take advantage of the information given to you."

She frowned, trying to figure out what he meant.

"I've told you about untold wealth, much that wouldn't go against your morals to own, and all you can focus on is that I've been waiting for centuries to be set free."

"What's wrong with that?" She felt uncomfortable with the way he looked at her. As if he examined her trying to figure her out.

"There's nothing wrong with it." His expression softened, along with his voice. "It's a nice change from what I am accustomed to." He chuckled. "And now you're uncomfortable again and I have no idea why."

She grinned. "You wouldn't understand." Turning away from him she got in the car before he had a chance to figure it out for himself. She hadn't exactly been uncomfortable. More at a loss as to how to react to his compliment and feeling awkward due to how close he stood and the interest in him she continually fought against.

Luca closed the door and walked around to the driver's side. He sat for a moment before he started the car, once again looking at her.

She wanted to ask him what he was thinking, but couldn't bring herself to speak. When he drove off, she asked, "Where are we going?"

"Southbank. I thought you might enjoy a walk along the river."

"That'd be nice."

They remained silent throughout the drive, neither speaking until they were walking along the riverbank. Penelope glanced in both directions. "It's more crowded than I expected."

"This way." He placed his hand against the middle of her back. "There are less people further down the river."

The crowd thinned and Penelope found a spot with no one nearby, stopping to look out across the river, the city lights reflected on the water. "It seems kind of magical." She turned so she could look at Luca. "I haven't believed in magic since I was a little kid."

"It exists. But not in the way of children's story books."

"In what way?"

"Those that call themselves wizards use demons or jinni to do their bidding." He remained silent for a moment. "You're not thinking of calling upon demons, are you?"

"No."

"Never call upon them. Not even the jinni. Most aren't like me. There's nothing human about them and they love to cause mischief."

"And you don't?"

Luca grinned. "I wouldn't exactly say that. But those I torment deserve the treatment." His head rose and his expression became serious as he looked around the area. "There are demons nearby. Two of them."

"How can you tell?"

"The same way they can tell I'm nearby once they're close enough." He put his arm around her waist. "They're closing in on us. Coming directly to our location. We need to leave the area."

It was a struggle to keep up with his stride, but she wasn't tempted to ask him to slow down. Maybe she'd seen too many horror movies, but demons weren't high on her list of things she wanted to meet.

Luca abruptly changed direction. "They're following us and coming in quick. We need to find some shadows."

"What for?"

He drew her into the shadows of a building and swung her up into his arms. "Close your eyes."

"Why?"

"It's less disorientating."

Closing her eyes, she felt a rush of air. Intrigued, she was about to open them when Luca spoke.

"Keep them closed. I can feel your curiosity."

"What would happen if I opened them?" She felt the rush of air stop.

"Open your eyes now." Luca set her down by the passenger door of her convertible. "We need to leave. They're coming in fast." He opened the door.

She looked back in the direction they'd been. "How did we get here so quickly?"

"We don't have time for this conversation. I need to take you somewhere safe."

She got in the car, watching as he closed the door and moved around to the driver's door in a blur of motion. Her mouth dropped open. No wonder he'd told her to close her eyes. She thought he'd moved fast previously, but it was nothing compared to the speed of his movements now. She waited until he was seated and the car was moving before she spoke, raising her voice to be heard above the rush of air through the broken window. "How can you see where you're going when you drive that fast?"

"Easily."

He hadn't really answered her question, but she didn't bother asking again even though she wanted to know. She had other concerns. "If you keep driving this fast we'll be pulled over."

"Cameras don't work on me. Even speed cameras. Which is why there are no pictures of me and no security camera footage."

"The police won't need a camera to tell them you're speeding. They'll be able to see." She clung to her seat, drawing her breath in sharply when they wove their way between traffic, some of it oncoming. "You'll get us killed."

"I will not get you killed and I can easily persuade the police. Did you forget about that ability?"

"You won't have that ability when you're human."

He glanced at her, grinning. "I often charmed people into my way of thinking, back when I was human."

She didn't doubt it and bet many of those he'd charmed were female.

Luca glanced at her again, a puzzled expression on his face. "Jealousy?"

"No." The word came out quicker than she'd planned.

Luca chuckled. "The emotion was too clear for you to lie about it."

She glanced out the window, but looked forward when the rush of scenery made her feel queasy. She wasn't normally car sick, but then she didn't usually go this fast. "Where are we going?"

"Sacred ground. Demons cannot enter it."

"Can you?"

"Yes. Jinni can, but not shayateen. Unless of course a jinn has become evil."

"How do you know where to find sacred land?"

"It's land that's been blessed."

She frowned, trying to figure out what he meant, confusion washing over her. She was so far out of her depth she had no idea about half of what was going on.

"You're not religious."

"No."

"That explains it." He pulled up in front of a graveyard, parking beside several other cars. "Blessed by priests. Like a church or a graveyard."

She stared at the fence separating them from the graveyard. "We're going in there?"

"You're not superstitious?" He was out of the car and opening her door before she could answer. "I'll protect you. I have no choice other than to protect you."

She got out of the car, looking over her shoulder, half expecting to see demons. Not that she knew what they looked like. "Have you faced demons before?"

"Once. Many years ago." He closed the door and placed a hand against the middle of her back, guiding her towards the graveyard.

"What happened?"

"That is a story for another day."

Stepping through the gate, she pulled away to turn and face him. "You lost, didn't you?"

"There was no sacred ground. You're safe here."

"I can't live in a graveyard."

Luca chuckled, placing his hand at her back and turning her in the direction they'd been walking. "The demons will vanish with the day."

"Why don't you?"

"Jinni are different to demons."

She pulled away from him in annoyance. "I don't know anything about all this so stop laughing at me."

"I wasn't laughing at you, Penelope. I was laughing

at the image you conjured with your words. I could never imagine you living on the streets." He faced her when she stopped walking, reaching out to run his hand along her cheek. "You are as far as it is possible to be from being a homeless person."

Her eyes narrowed. "Is that an insult?"

"Neither insult nor compliment. Merely a statement of fact."

She looked over his shoulder. Before she could mention the man walking towards them along the shadowy path, Luca was facing him, his body blocking her view.

"I'm surprised he sent you," Luca said.

"I have just as much to lose," the man said.

"Who is he?" Penelope peered around Luca's body.

"The son of the man who wishes my return." Luca raised his voice. "Come no closer. I have no reason to let you live."

The man stopped. "I want to talk to your new master."

"What about?" She remained shielded by Luca's body, not trusting the man in front of them. Even in his ordinary looking business suit, with neatly styled brown hair that was slightly thinning, he looked like a thug. She didn't know if it was because of his stance, his broad shoulders, his expression or a combination of all three.

"You only need to be clinically dead for a few seconds for Luca to be set free," the man said. "Agree to willingly let us have him back and we'll have medical staff on hand to resuscitate you as soon as we have control of him again."

"I don't trust you."

"Tell her, Luca," the man ordered.

"Chad and his father will keep their word."

She felt a moment of fear, followed by resignation. It came from Luca. She placed her hand against his back, remaining behind him. "Why the demons?"

"To track Luca down. Once Luca is no longer bound to you, they'll return to where they came from," Chad said. "What's your answer?"

"She needs time to think on it. You're asking her to die," Luca said.

"She really only has two options. Die for a few seconds or die permanently. We're willing to do whatever it takes to regain control of you," Chad warned.

"Twenty-four hours," Luca said.

Chad took out his phone. "I'll give you until ten tomorrow night. Close enough to twenty-four hours." He returned his phone to his suit pocket.

"You know my number." He gave a single nod before turning and heading towards the entrance.

Chapter Eight

Penelope watched Chad leave, continuing to hide behind Luca, leaning against him. "I don't want to die."

"I know."

"And I don't want him to have you. I don't like him."

"We'll discuss it during the day. When there are no demons about that might overhear." He turned to face her.

She stepped back so she wasn't plastered all over his chest. "What are we going to do now?"

"Find somewhere comfortable to wait out the night." He placed his hand against her back and headed further into the graveyard.

She pulled away from him. "We're staying here?" It was darker further away from the entrance. The streetlights didn't cast their light that far.

"Do you really wish to go home and lead the demons to your family? For now they don't know who you are or where you live. I thought you might wish to keep it that way."

"We need to break the curse. Before the week is up."

"They'll not give up. Now they've involved demons things are more dangerous for you."

She turned her back on him, resignation creeping over her. She should have expected something like this. Even that which was meant to be hers forever would be taken from her before she was ready.

Luca stepped close, the warmth of his body radiating against hers. "We could run, but you would need to spend the rest of your life running. Or you could send me after Chad and Eugene. Once they're dead no one would know what I am. No one would have any reason to come after you."

"No."

"No to which option."

"Neither. We set you free."

"That might not stop them. They're likely to want revenge. I have a way to stop them, but they may take their revenge before I can implement it."

"I'll take my chances." When he continued to stare at her, she demanded, "What?" There were too many shadows for her to see his expression. Not that it would have helped. He was far better than her at being expressionless.

"You would risk your life for me? I am no one to you."

It took her nearly a minute to answer. "It doesn't feel that way."

"How does it feel?" His voice was whisper soft.

She slowly shook her head, turning her back on him. She knew a little of how he must feel. His wishes of no interest to anyone. "It doesn't matter." She glared at him when he moved in front of her, a blur of motion. "Will you stop doing that? It's…" She struggled to think of the right word.

"Unnatural?"

"No. Startling." She pressed her hand against his chest, until he stepped back. "How are we meant to find somewhere comfortable in a graveyard?"

"Don't move." He was gone in a blur of motion.

She slowly turned around, trying to see where he was. It had been a bad idea. Her scan of the area showed her numerous moving shadows, which might have been trees and shrubs or could have been something coming after her. Another movement caught her attention and she turned towards it, her hand pressed against her heart, the other against her mouth to keep a scream from escaping.

"What is wrong?"

She lowered her hands. "Stop sneaking up on me like that."

"I've found somewhere comfortable. Or at least as comfortable as we're likely to find in a graveyard." He held out his hand. "Do you want me to take you there?"

She shook her head. "I'll walk."

He lowered his hand, inclining his head. "This way."

She walked beside him, through the graveyard, to a timber slat bench. Sitting down she looked past the far fence to the road beyond. Traffic occasionally passed, the road mostly quiet. "It's going to be a long night."

He sat beside her and took her hand. "Is there something I can do to help the time pass more quickly?"

She stared at their hands, his larger than hers, his skin several shades darker than her own. "What were your family like?" When he remained silent, she looked towards him, trying to make out his expression in the light cast from the streetlights lining the road. "Do you remember them after all this time?"

"Like it was yesterday." He fell silent a moment longer before he began to speak.

She listened as he spoke of his brothers and the many adventures they'd gone on and the trouble they'd often ended up in. She smiled at the fondness in his voice, the regular touches of sorrow. "You care about them. After all this time you still care about them."

"I never had the chance to say goodbye. We had so little time together."

She had no idea what to say so remained silent, glad the night was warm. Eventually her name being spoken had her blinking sleepily up at Luca, early morning light making it easier to see his expression. He was smiling at her. "I fell asleep?"

Luca chuckled. "Like someone put out a candle." He paused a moment. "We can go home."

She glanced around the area, noticing there were more cars going past. "The demons have gone?"

Luca nodded. "With the sunrise. They were too powerful to remain during the day. They'll be back at sunset."

"We need to ring that number to contact Emily. It's in my handbag at home." She stumbled to her feet, feeling half asleep.

Luca steadied her. "You can have a couple more hours sleep first. You look tired."

She walked beside him towards her convertible. "Is that your way of telling me I look terrible?"

"No. It would take far more than lack of sleep for that."

She glanced towards him, then away, trying not to smile and to keep her emotions neutral. It was odd knowing he could sense her emotions at times. Reaching the vehicle, she got in the passenger side, nowhere near awake enough to drive. She drifted off to sleep again, blinking several times when Luca gently shook her. It took her nearly a minute before she could focus enough to get out of the car and head towards her bedroom, Luca at her side.

"Are you only now getting in?"

Penelope turned around to see her mother step into the hallway. She glanced to where Luca had been, looking over her shoulder when she didn't see him.

"Is something the matter?"

"No." She looked past her mother. Where had Luca gone? Vanishing hadn't been on the list of things he'd said he could do.

"Where did you go?"

"Dinner. I saw Harrison and Suzie."

"That's nice." Her mother checked the time. "I'll see you later."

Penelope stared after her mother, guessing she hadn't seen Luca. So where was he? She glanced around the hallway once more before heading to her room. She stopped in the doorway, staring at him seated in the armchair. "How did you get here? You vanished."

"I'm not capable of turning invisible. I didn't know if you wanted your mother to see you coming in with me, after being out all night, so I moved away when I heard her approaching."

Shrugging, she closed the door. "It doesn't matter."

Luca crossed the room in a second, taking her hands. "That makes you sad?"

"Not exactly." She tried to think of a way to explain, but was too tired. "She'd approve of you. The way you talk and carry yourself would make her think you might be someone important."

"Do you think I am not? My family was one of the few whose patent of creation allowed all male heirs to inherit the title, not only the oldest son."

"Okay." She was about to step past him when she felt his amusement. "Why are you laughing at me?"

"I'm not laughing. You have no idea what that means, do you?"

She shrugged. "Something important I guess." The continued amusement she felt from him caused annoyance to rise in her. She brushed past him. "I'm going to bed." She headed to the ensuite first, finding Luca sitting in the armchair when she came out. Remaining in the doorway, she stared at him. Jumbled thoughts filled her mind and she tried to keep her emotions neutral. She feared Luca might notice she was worried. "What are you going to do when you're set free? Other than visit your old home."

Luca shrugged. "I'll decide after I visit."

She fleetingly felt his longing, surprised he wasn't as guarded with his emotions as he had been the night they'd met. "You want to stay nearby."

"It will have changed."

"But you want it to be the home you remember and you're not going to decide anything until you know for certain."

Luca crossed the room in a blur of motion. "How did you work that out?"

"Because I sometimes do the same." Going after the dog had been a waste of time. Even if he'd been at the RSPCA her mother wouldn't have let her bring him home. But she'd had to try anyway. Had hoped there'd be some way to figure things out.

Luca started to reach for her, stepping back instead. "If you're tired you should have a sleep. We'll contact the hunters later."

It was a moment before she could nod and cross the room to her bed, slipping between the sheets. She watched as he returned to the armchair, his gaze eventually meeting hers. Having no idea why, she smiled at him before she closed her eyes and sank into sleep.

Her dreams were filled with demons, guns and running. She tossed and turned, her sleep less restful than what she'd had in the graveyard. It was almost a relief when a knock on her bedroom door dragged her from her nightmares. She stumbled out of bed, waving Luca back to the armchair he'd been sitting on. Sleepiness vanished when she saw who was at her door. "No." She glared at the woman who held a clipboard with notes and paint chips.

"It is so lovely to see you, Penelope." The woman smiled, her voice friendly.

"No, it's not." She continued to glare at the woman.

"It has been such a very long time. I hear you graduated from year twelve last year." The woman's smile didn't slip and her tone remained friendly.

"Five months. Not long enough." She fought

against the anger that rose, shaking her head with a glance towards Luca when he stood up.

"Your mother is intrigued by a style I call stately forties. Elegant and classy, drawing on some of the colours of the forties such as these lovely blues and greens." The woman indicated the colour chips on her clipboard.

"I already said no. I like my room exactly the way it is."

"You say that every time. As always I am certain the new look will grow on you."

"It won't. I don't like those colours."

The woman laughed lightly. A high, false note. "You say that every time too. You know you'll love the new look within weeks and be thrilled with the changes."

Resignation washed over her. "What do you want?"

"Why to check a couple of measurements. It's always best to be certain of these things."

Penelope glanced towards Luca who remained out of the woman's sight. "Come back later. I haven't finished sleeping. Besides, with the amount of times you've redecorated the house you should know all of the dimensions by heart."

The woman pressed her hand against the door. "I

won't be more than a moment. Then you can return to sleep and I can begin the planning stage. Your mother wants this dealt with immediately."

Anger rushed through Penelope, pushing away the resignation. "I said later." She shoved at the door, locking it the moment she managed to get it closed.

Chapter Nine

Penelope leaned against the door, watching Luca who came to stand in front of her.

"I'll make sure you have your week."

"No. It's crazy. We'll break the curse as soon as possible. If anything happened to me-"

"Nothing will happen to you. I will not allow it."

Her lips twisted into a smile. "That isn't what you were saying last night." She pressed her fingers against his lips when he tried to speak again. "It's okay. You don't want to risk being under the control of your old master. I don't want you under his control."

He took her hand, lowering it and keeping hold of it. "Does anyone listen to what you want?"

She sighed, her gaze shifting to the side. When he remained silent, obviously waiting for her answer, she looked at him again. "No."

"You can have your week."

"I don't want it anymore." She pressed her other hand against his lips when he started to speak again. "You're not listening to me."

He smiled, his lips moving against her fingers before he took hold of that hand with his other, lowering it too. "Tell me this is what you really want."

She met his gaze, the piercing blue of his eyes more intense than usual. "This is what I want." It was the right thing to do. She shouldn't have asked for a week. That had been wrong.

"Then why does it feel like it isn't? Why do I sense regret?"

"For making you wait so long to be free. It was selfish of me. I shouldn't have done it."

"Are you certain you don't want a week?"

She pushed away her regrets, trying to figure out what kind of emotion she should be feeling. Happy? Satisfied? Determined? She had no idea. "I'm positive."

Luca chuckled. "I don't believe you. Not after the mix of emotions you shoved at me. But I would be a fool to argue."

She squeezed his hands tightly. "If anything

happened and they got you back I'd regret it for the rest of my life. That is something I can't live with."

He slowly nodded. "That I can believe. Your emotions finally match your words."

"What emotions?"

"Fierceness. Protectiveness."

"Oh."

He smiled, squeezing her hands in return. "Ring Father Joe and have him pass your number along to Emily."

She held onto his hands a little longer, not wanting to let go. Emily should have given her a direct number. She didn't want to talk to a priest. Letting go, she collected the handbag from her walk-in wardrobe and took out the card. One edge was bent and she smoothed it out before dialling the number.

"Father Joe."

"Uhm, hi. This is Penelope G-" She broke off, wondering if she should give him her last name.

"How can I help you, Penelope?"

He sounded young. Too young to be a priest. "Emily told me to leave my number with you and she'd ring me back."

"I'm afraid Emily can't be contacted today. There's no mobile phone reception where she is."

"What about Dan?"

"He's with her."

"Oh." Dropping the card on the bed, she started to pace.

"Is there something I can help you with? They had to go away unexpectedly."

"No. Can you get Emily to ring me the moment she has reception?"

"I can, but are you sure I can't help you? What was it about?"

She twisted a lock of her hair between her fingers. There was no way she could tell him. "I'll give you my number."

"One moment while I find pen and paper."

She listened to Father Joe rummage around, letting go of her hair when she realised what she was doing.

"Ready."

She rattled off her number, listening as he repeated it. "You'll have her ring as soon as possible, won't you?"

"Of course, but there–"

"Thanks. Tell her to call at any hour." She said goodbye, hanging up once Father Joe had once more failed to find out what she wanted. There was no way she was going to tell someone else her problems. What if he thought she was crazy and didn't pass along her message? Emily hadn't said he knew anything about demons. Only to leave a message with him.

"We need to leave Brisbane before dark. If we keep moving the demons might not be able to lead Chad to us before morning."

"Is that all we have to do to avoid the demons? Keep moving?"

"No. They are a little more difficult to avoid than that. They can move a great deal faster than a car. At least for short periods of time."

"Like you can."

He inclined his head.

"You could outrun them." When he again nodded, she asked, "Why don't you leave me behind?"

"You are my master, Exalted One. I could more easily die permanently than leave you in danger."

She remembered his words when she'd told him he'd die. 'Not permanently. The curse will not allow it.' She struggled to find words. None made sense. Just like the situation. "I have to get ready." She strode to the walk-in wardrobe and grabbed her clothes before heading to the ensuite. A shower didn't help. Stepping into her room she stood awkwardly in front of him, fighting the urge to play with her hair, having no idea what to say.

"You're ready?"

She began to nod, shaking her head instead. "I need to pack some clothes. Who knows how long it'll take to reach…" She frowned, trying to remember where they had to go. "The place where the medallion has to be put back together."

"The resting place of Solomon."

Her frown returned. "Isn't he some bible man?"

Luca inclined his head. "He was a king of Israel."

"Did you know him?"

Luca chuckled. "I'm not that old. He was the king around 970 to 931 BC."

"Oh." She looked away, gesturing towards her walk-in wardrobe. "I better get some things together."

"We will travel light."

She fled to the walk-in wardrobe, closing the door behind her, trying to keep her emotions neutral as she leaned back against the door. He must think her an idiot. But she knew nothing about the bible. Only what she'd seen in movies or references she'd come across in other books. And history had never interested her. No, the things that had interested her hadn't been suitable and she hadn't been allowed to pursue them.

Shoving clothes in a large cloth handbag, she tried not to think of the many arguments she'd had with her parents when she was younger. Until she'd realised that she was wasting her time and no one would listen no matter what she said or how loudly she said it.

She slung the bag over her shoulder and opened the door. "I'm ready."

Luca took the bag from her and stepped out of her room. They were nearly at the garage when Luca began to move away from her.

Expecting it to be one of her parents, she spoke quietly, knowing it would be impossible to catch him before he disappeared from sight. "Stay with me."

He returned to her side with the same fast movement, turning to face the other direction.

She slowly turned, seeing her mother walking towards her.

"Are you going to introduce me to your friend?"

"This is Luca Simoneti." She spoke quickly, worried he might say he was an Italian count.

"You have Italian heritage?" Penelope's mother asked.

Luca inclined his head. "It is nice to meet you, Mrs Grayson."

"You're going out?"

Penelope nodded. "We're going away for a few

days." She nearly smiled at the shock she saw in her mother's eyes before she managed to mask it.

"The two of you? Alone?"

Penelope was tempted to say yes to see what her mother's reaction would be. "A group of us are going." That was if she could get hold of Emily and Dan.

"Will Harrison be going with you?"

"Didn't I tell you? Harrison and I are over. He's with Suzie now." Again she momentarily saw shock in her mother's eyes.

"I thought you might last longer. That you'd finally decided not to flit from one thing to another."

Anger rushed through her and she forced it back. There'd been things she hadn't wanted to 'flit' away from. But they hadn't been appropriate.

"We'd best leave. We do not want to be caught in heavy traffic or be late meeting up with the rest of the group." Luca held out his hand.

Penelope's mother shook his hand before facing her daughter. "Ring and let me know when you've arrived and where you're staying."

Penelope nodded, unable to speak from the anger she continued to fight against. She turned away and headed towards the garage. Her anger hadn't gone by the time they reached the car and she glared at the passenger door Luca held open. "It's my car."

"I know."

"Then I'll drive."

"If you want. We need to go to my house first."

Surprise pushed the anger away. "Your house?"

Luca smiled. "Do you want me to drive?"

She sat heavily in the seat. "You have a house?" How was that possible? Hadn't he needed to stay with his master all the time?

He closed the door and strode around to the driver's side. Once he'd put the bag on the back seat, he started the car. "I learned to outsource some of the jobs Eugene wanted done. It gave me time to spend as I wished. Some jobs it wasn't possible to pay others to do."

"And the house?"

"I needed somewhere private to stay."

"Does Eugene or Chad know about it?"

"No."

She tried to figure out the fleeing emotion she'd felt from him. "Is it far?"

"You'll have all your questions about the house answered soon enough."

"No I won't."

He glanced towards her. "Why is that?"

"Seeing it won't tell me why you're letting me know about it." She watched him, waiting for an answer that never came. "Luca?"

He glanced towards her again, this time saying nothing.

"Why are you taking me to your house?"

"You'll be safe there if you should have need of somewhere to hide."

"What about you? Where will you be?"

There was a lengthy silence before he spoke. "I want you to have somewhere safe to go if things should go wrong. They don't know you and the demons cannot track you without your blood. I'm currently the only one they can track."

"You're leaving me there?" She wanted to beg him not to desert her.

"That worries you?"

She tried to reign in her emotions. They were replaced with resignation. "Do what you want." She looked out the window, glad her voice hadn't reflected the resignation she felt. It had been unconcerned. A tone she'd had plenty of practice at.

"If I did as I wanted, you would probably slap me."

Startled by his words, she stared at him. She nearly asked him to explain what he meant by his words, but at the last second her courage failed her. "I guess there's only one way to know for sure."

Luca glanced at her, grinning. "There's more than one way to know for sure. You could tell me instead of letting me risk finding out the hard way."

Chapter Ten

Penelope opened her mouth, determined to ask Luca exactly what he meant. The words remained unspoken when he glanced towards her again and she caught a glimpse of the look in his eyes. Her heart raced, needing no explanation as to his meaning. Her gaze was drawn to his lips that curved into a smile. Swallowing hard, she looked away. She was setting him free. It'd be madness getting involved when he planned on leaving the moment the curse was broken. It took her a moment to realise she was twisting a strand of her hair between her fingers. She let it go.

"You're uncomfortable again."

There was no point in denying it so she remained quiet, continuing to do so for the rest of the drive. When they pulled up in the driveway of a large house, she checked the time and saw it had only taken them half an hour to arrive. She stared at the two-storey building that had a slight castle like look to it with its rendered exterior and bay windows that went the full height of the building.

Luca came around and opened her door, continuing to hold it when she remained seated. "Did you want to wait out here? I can turn the air-conditioner back on."

"No." She wanted to see his place. She followed him inside, the coolness of the interior washing over her when she stepped in out of the sun. "Who lives here with you?"

"No one."

"Are you sure?" The place was pretty large for one person and it didn't have the unlived in feeling she'd expected.

"I have someone come in once a week to keep it tidy."

"Oh." She hadn't expected that.

Luca faced her, standing within reach. "Why does all this make you feel uncomfortable?"

"Will you come back here once you've visited your family home?"

"I don't know."

"Why don't you know?"

"This is only a house."

"And the castle is home?"

"It was once." He paused a moment. "I have to collect a few things before we run out of daylight. I don't want to be anywhere near this house when demons track us down."

She followed him through the house, stopping when he did. She watched as he keyed a code into a number pad beside a door. Her mouth dropped open when Luca entered the room. "You have an arsenal?" She stared at the weapons stored in the room, a mixture of medieval and modern.

Luca took down a sword from where it was displayed, gathering daggers and a gun. "Why does this surprise you?"

She didn't know why, but it did. She followed him out of the room. "What are you planning on doing with the weapons?"

"Protecting you."

Her gaze was drawn to the gun. "You're going to shoot someone?"

"I cannot go against your orders and kill anyone."

"But you'll shoot them."

Luca faced her. "What would you have me do? Be shot instead?"

She shook her head, not liking that option either.

"Why do you need the sword and daggers if you have a gun?"

"The gun will be useless when we travel to the resting place of Solomon."

She opened her mouth several times before she managed to speak. "It'll be dangerous." She felt his amusement wash over her.

He grinned. "Did you expect anything else?"

Sighing heavily, she looked away from his gaze, uncomfortable once more. "I had no idea what to expect."

He tucked the gun in the back of his waistband, reaching out to lightly brush his fingers across her cheek. "What is wrong, Penelope? Have you changed your mind?"

She met his gaze, looking into his blue eyes, seeing a similar resignation to the one she frequently felt. "You don't think I'll go through with this."

"You don't know what to expect. The danger you will face. You'll need to be there to give permission for the curse to be broken. You will have to stand in the resting place of Solomon and say I am no longer bound to you. That my debt is paid."

She stepped closer, placing her hand against his heart, feeling the steady beat beneath her palm. "I will set you free. No matter what I have to face." She tried not to think about the fact he planned to leave the moment he was free.

"That pains you?"

She shook her head, trying to swallow past the lump in her throat.

"You cannot lie to me about what you feel. I sensed your pain as clearly as if I were the one who felt it."

"The thought of setting you free doesn't cause pain." She fought the urge to twist a strand of hair between her fingers.

Luca frowned. "Then what pains you and why would that question make you feel uncomfortable?"

Lowering her hand, she turned away from him. She'd once been far better at keeping her emotions in check. Luca was destroying years of practice. "You'll leave." Feeling his shock, she spun to face him, a smile half forming. "Surprised? Maybe you're not as good at sensing my emotions as you thought."

"Maybe I've feared it was my own emotions, not yours." He reached for her with one hand, drawing her close, the other continuing to hold his sword and daggers. "You don't make a very good master." His lips met hers.

The question she'd been about to ask vanished and she slid her hands around his neck, returning his kiss. When he drew away slightly, she met his gaze. "I have no desire to be anyone's master." She tried to think of the question she'd wanted to ask. It was gone.

"As difficult as that is to comprehend, I believe you."

"Why is it so difficult?"

He ran his fingers lightly across her cheek. "All who've learned what I am have made it their mission to control me. Have coveted the power I could give them."

"I have no power, but I don't want power by putting someone else in the same situation I've always been in."

"When all this is over it will be my turn to set you free."

"I'm not imprisoned."

"Do you really think that?"

Before she could argue his comment, her phone rang. Checking the display, she saw it was her mother. Sighing, she answered the phone. "We haven't reached our destination yet. Haven't even left the city."

"I can't believe you'd defy me like this."

"What?"

"Your grandmother will be here this evening. This will be worse than the ninja episode."

"What will?"

"Do not play dumb with me. Return the dog to the RSPCA. I don't have time for this."

"The dog?"

"Penelope Elizabeth Grayson you will stop this charade immediately. If you don't return home and deal with the situation I will and you'll not like it."

When her mother hung up, she stared at the phone. "My dog is back?"

"What was the ninja episode?"

"Uhm, it doesn't matter. I was a little kid." She slowly shook her head. "What am I going to do with him?"

"Bring him here. Put him in the backyard."

"I–" Words failed her. She had no idea what to think. A smile slowly formed. "He came back to me." Nothing like this had ever happened to her before.

"You're obviously worth returning to."

She was surprised by the fierce feeling that washed over her. Surprised and confused. "Am I?" She wanted to ask him if he'd return to her after he'd visited his family's home.

"Don't let the way others see you effect how you see yourself."

She nearly told him it was too late for that. Far too late. "I have to get my dog before my mother does something drastic." She sent a text to say she'd be half an hour.

"You need to go alone. It is too close to dark. I'll not lead them to you."

"You're deserting me?" She took a step backwards.

He followed, taking her hand. "Never. I'll lead them away so you can safely collect your dog and bring him here." He smiled. "And tomorrow you'll tell me about the ninja episode."

"Uhm… no."

"Yes. With how uncomfortable talking about it makes you feel, I'm intrigued."

She glanced away from his stare. "How will I contact you if I need you?"

"I'll organise a phone for myself and call you with the number."

"You don't have my number."

"I memorised it when you told the priest." He held out the key he'd used to unlock the front door. "Be careful. Come straight back here where it's safe."

"Okay."

He half turned away. Facing her again, he drew her close for another kiss. He started to say something, smiling instead before he walked away.

She stood there a moment, feeling slightly dazed. How had life changed so quickly? Taking a deep breath, she pushed her emotions aside and headed for the car. Her dog needed to be rescued. Everything else could be figured out later.

When she arrived home it was to find the dog had been tied up by the back door and the housekeeper had fed him some scraps. Penelope thanked the woman.

The housekeeper glanced over her shoulder. "It might be best to walk around the house to your car. Your mother isn't in a good mood."

"I guessed that." She untied the rope. "I'll send her a text to let her know I've collected him."

The housekeeper nodded, remaining in the doorway.

The dog jumped up on Penelope once he was untied and she knelt to wrap her arms around him, whispering into his matted fur. "I missed you too." Reluctantly letting go, she stood up.

"A dog like that," the housekeeper gestured towards him, "he'll be loyal forever." She paused a moment. "A pity more people aren't like him."

Penelope wasn't about to argue that statement. "I better go." She didn't want to risk running into her mother.

The housekeeper nodded. "That'd be best."

She hurried to the front of the house, the dog

jumping around beside her. Worried his enthusiastic behaviour might not be good in the front of the car, she put him on the back seat. Once she was seated, he rested his head on her shoulder and she couldn't stop grinning all the way to Luca's house.

When they arrived, she searched around for something to use to wash the dog. She found a bar of soap in the downstairs bathroom. The dog was dirty, his fur matted and he looked a little thin. He stared at her mournfully while she washed him, but didn't try to escape, showering her with water once she was finished.

"You need a name."

The dog barked.

"Any preferences?" When he rested his head against her knee, she patted him. "How does Rusty sound?"

Again the dog barked.

"Rusty it is." She rubbed his head. "Although I should call you Houdini. How did you get away and how did you find your way back to me?"

He licked her hand.

Smiling, she strode to the back patio and sat at the table, continuing to pat Rusty when he joined her. She remained seated on the patio as darkness fell and the day cooled off slightly. "What am I going to do with you?" There was no way her mother would let her keep him. And there was no way she could let him go. He was hers and he'd returned to her.

Chapter Eleven

Penelope's phone rang and she checked the display. She didn't recognise the number. "Hello?"

"What is wrong?" Luca demanded.

"Nothing."

"Your joy became that fierce protective feeling. What is wrong?"

"I can't give him up. He came back to me."

"The dog."

"Rusty."

"You named him."

"Yes." When he remained silent, she asked. "Are you okay?"

"The demons are following me. Chad wants to be prepared for whatever choice you make."

"I'm not going to change my mind. He can't have you. I'm setting you free." When he laughed, she asked, "What's so funny?"

"That was the same feeling you had when you wanted to keep Rusty."

She had no idea what to say. Knowing there was no one who could see her, she gave into the urge to twist a strand of hair between her fingers.

"What is wrong? You're uncomfortable again."

"How can you sense how I feel when you're not near me?"

"You could be on the other side of the world and I would know how you felt. If you weren't trying to hide it." He chuckled. "And you're uncomfortable again."

"This isn't fair. I'm usually a lot better at hiding how I feel." She patted Rusty when he whined, pressing his damp nose against her hand. "Could I sense how you feel from this distance?"

"You should be able to."

"But you're hiding it." Before she could complain again about how unfair it was, a flood of feelings washed over her. She was glad she was sitting down. She tried to untangle the various feelings before the flood ended abruptly. "Protective?" She frowned. That didn't seem exactly right.

"Amongst other things."

"What other things?"

There was silence for a moment before Luca spoke.

"The demons are closing in. I need to go. Ring if you need me. There's food in the fridge and cupboards."

"I can't cook."

He chuckled. "I should have known. There's money in the weapons room. I'll text you the code and you can order takeaway."

He was gone before she had a chance to say anything else. What did it mean that the demons were closing in? He had to be safe.

While her phone was in her hand, she decided to send a text to her mother. *Have arrived safely. Will let you know when we reach our next destination.* Hopefully that would be enough information for now that her mother wouldn't ask where she was. It'd probably help that her grandmother was there making a nuisance of herself.

Leaving Rusty outside, after filling a bucket with water, she wandered through the house, trying to gain a better understanding of Luca. There were books stacked on a side table beside an armchair, medieval looking artefacts on shelves, a painting of his family's castle hanging in the lounge room and suits hanging in the walk-in wardrobe in the master bedroom. It made her sad to see them until she found a box. It was tucked away at the back of the walk-in wardrobe, containing a pair of medieval boots she feared to touch in case they fell apart.

He'd go home and she'd be surprised if he ever returned. He'd wanted to go home for centuries. Returning the box to where she'd found it, she checked on Rusty. He was lying in front of the back door, his tail wagging when he spotted her. At least her dog had returned. She bent to pat him before she went inside and called for takeaway. When it arrived, she paid for it with her own money, not wanting a reminder of how harsh Luca's life had been. A fierce protectiveness raced through her. She'd only spent eighteen years having her wishes ignored. What would it have felt like going through that for centuries?

Her phone beeped and she checked the message, smiling as she read Luca's text.

Were you thinking of me or the dog?

She debated replying. In the end she decided to answer. *You.* She stumbled at the strength of the emotions that washed over her. Was that for her or for the fact she cared about him? She didn't know and didn't have the courage to ask.

After she'd eaten, sitting on the patio with Rusty and sharing the food with him, she returned to wandering around the house. Several times she was tempted to call Luca to see how he was. Each time she decided not to, worried she might distract him and put him in more danger.

Dropping into his armchair she reached for one of the books, flicking through it sightlessly. She'd learned one thing from this night. She wasn't the type to sit at home waiting. Whatever she ended up doing with her life it wasn't going to be anything to do with waiting around for long periods of time. She didn't have the patience for it. Not that she knew what else she could do.

A wry smile formed. Being a ninja wasn't an option. She hoped Luca forgot about her mother's comment, but she had a feeling his memory was far better than hers. Look at how easily he'd memorised her number. She was still thinking of him when she drifted off to sleep, woken hours later by Luca picking her up.

"It's morning?" She blinked up at him, cradled in his arms.

He strode upstairs. "The sun rose an hour ago."

"Did you contact Chad?"

"Yes." He placed her on the bed.

"What did you tell him?"

"Not interested."

She reached for him when he started to move

away, tugging him back. "What did he say?" When he didn't answer, she drew him down so that he sat beside her. "Luca?"

"It'll be the second option then."

"Anything else?"

Luca shrugged. "I hung up before he could say another word."

She didn't want to die.

Luca gathered her in his arms. "He will not touch you. Nor will his demons."

"What about when you're no longer a jinn?"

"When they can no longer follow me of an evening I can gather some of the proof I've collected, over the years, of what they've done. I can send him a digital copy, but he'll expect at least a couple of the original copies. They'll leave us alone if they don't want the police to learn the details."

"You expected to escape?"

"I've done this for centuries. Kept details I could use to protect myself against retaliation if I should ever be freed."

She turned her head so she could see his face better. "Didn't you ever want to give up?"

"Of course."

"Then why didn't you?"

"I am Conte Luca Martino Simoneti. My family would be appalled if I was so weak as to give up."

She smiled at the pride she felt. "It means a lot to you. Your name. Your family."

It was a moment before he nodded, meeting her gaze. "They're a family worth being proud of."

"I wish I had a family worth being proud of." They weren't proud of her either.

"It starts with being proud of yourself. And goes down through the generations from that. If you don't have a family to be proud of, you create one."

"I like that idea." She yawned, trying to fight the urge.

"Sleep. When you wake you can tell me all about the ninja episode."

A smile reluctantly formed. She'd been right. He hadn't forgotten. She snuggled against him, her arms sliding around him. "It's not that interesting." Her eyes closed and she listened to the beat of his heart against her ear.

"You might be surprised at what I find interesting."

His words were soft and she doubted he expected a reply. She gave him one anyway. "Loyalty and family." She smiled when she felt surprise wash over her, drifting off to sleep in his arms.

When she woke, it was to find him lying beside her, holding her hand. "I thought you didn't sleep."

"You protested every time I tried to leave the bed."

"So you stayed?"

"Yes."

"I have to buy food for Rusty."

"I bought some on the way home this morning and fed him before I carried you up here."

"Oh."

"That surprises you?"

"I didn't expect it." She wasn't used to people anticipating her needs.

"Are you going to tell me about the ninja episode?"

"You'll keep asking until I do, won't you?"

"Unless you order me not to."

She grinned. "Then you'll ask me once I can no longer order you around."

He chuckled. "You have to admit it's not the usual comment a mother makes."

Sighing, she looked away from him. "I was six-years-old." And under the impression she could convince her parents if she tried hard enough. "I'd watched a highly inappropriate movie at a friend's house."

"Inappropriate?"

"Full of action, fighting and ninjas."

"Ah. For a moment I thought it was a different kind of inappropriate."

"I think they'd have almost preferred that." She paused a moment as she remembered the shock on her grandmother's face. "I cut up a set of black sheets and wrapped them around me mummy fashion. Then I cut out ninja stars from cardboard and coloured them silver with a crayon. By the time I'd finished I'd used up the entire crayon. I came running into the dining room, throwing my ninja stars. One of them hit my grandmother in the face."

Luca chuckled. "I take it she wasn't amused."

"She was so far from amused that she threatened to gain custody of me rather than have me raised so inappropriately. When I said I wanted to be a ninja they looked horrified. I was never allowed to visit that friend again and for years after, every time I did something inappropriate, my mother would remind me that my grandmother would make me live with her."

"You would have made a good ninja."

She met his gaze, smiling ruefully. "You don't have to tell me that to make me feel better."

"That fierce protective feeling I often sense from you, that tells me you'd have made a good ninja. Or any other warrior you might wish to be."

"Really?"

"Yes."

She looked away again. "It doesn't matter. There are no ninjas and even if there were, it's too late now."

He turned her face to him. "It's never too late. When you decide what you want to do, not what your family wants you to do, then you follow that path regardless of how inappropriate they think it is. Their view on life isn't the only one."

She drew him to her. "I don't know that I have your courage." She kissed him before he could argue.

When he eventually drew away, he smiled down at her. "You have more courage than you think." He left the bed in a blur of motion, holding out his hand. "Would you like me to make breakfast since you're unable to cook."

She took his hand, allowing him to tug her to her feet. "Yes. While you're doing that I'll have a shower then call the priest again."

Chapter Twelve

After Penelope showered and called the priest, she joined Luca on the patio where breakfast was set out on the table. "Emily and Dan haven't returned." She stared at the food in front of her, not really seeing it. "What are we going to do?"

"You can stay here and I'll lead them away like I did last night. It works well. You'll be safe."

"No. I can't sit here all night while you risk your life out there. I need to know what's going on, not pace the rooms of your house waiting for you to come home."

Luca stared at her for a moment before he nodded. "Eat your breakfast. We'll leave shortly."

"What about Rusty?"

"He'll be fine here. I'll send a text to the one who takes care of my house and let him know Rusty is here and to check on him while we're gone."

"Okay."

As soon as breakfast was eaten, and she'd said goodbye to Rusty, Luca led her to a four-wheel-drive parked in his garage, a sports car beside it. She grinned when she saw the sleek vehicle.

"Something amuses you?"

She nodded towards the sports car as she clambered in the four-wheel-drive. "I should have known you'd own a car like that. Especially with the way you drive."

He closed her door, a smile fleetingly appearing before he walked around to the driver's side. "I don't always drive like that. Only when my master is being chased." He started the vehicle, reversing out of the garage once the electric roller door had finished rising, and headed north.

Her good feeling evaporated.

"What is wrong?"

She looked out the window at the passing scenery. "I don't like that word."

Luca was silent for a moment. "Master?"

"Yeah. It's wrong." It reminded her of how she'd been unwilling to initially set him free. When the silence stretched out, she began to feel uncomfortable. She'd expected him to say something. Anything.

"What is wrong?"

She smiled at his words. They hadn't been what she'd expected. "You ask that a lot."

He glanced towards her. "You so rarely feel joy."

"I do. Sometimes."

"What was the last thing you felt joy about?"

Grinning, she looked at him.

He glanced at her again. "That didn't include me. Or Rusty."

She tried to think, frowning when nothing came to mind. Her frown cleared. "We went to France last year. Friends of my parents were married over there. Everyone was so busy celebrating that they didn't notice me wander off to explore the city on my own."

"What did you like most about it?"

"No one knew me. There was no one to run to my parents with tales of how inappropriate I was behaving." She grinned. "I did all the touristy things and found so many interesting places. It was great not feeling like someone was always looking over my shoulder waiting to point out what I was doing wrong." Her grin vanished. "No one knew I'd wandered off. The talk was all about the wedding and reception and how perfect it had been."

"Have you been to other places?"

She nodded, talking about the handful of countries

she'd visited with her family, asking him about the many places he'd been. She listened to the stories he told about places and how they grew and changed. Some he'd returned to, others he only knew of them as they'd been in the past. They stopped for something to eat late afternoon and as the light faded from the sky, they pulled up at a deserted beach, having driven through a narrow track that meandered through bushland.

"Why are we stopping?"

"There were only two demons last night. On my own I was able to keep one step ahead of them. With you at my side I'll need to face them."

"What do you mean face them?" When he got out of the vehicle without answering, she clambered out too, joining him at the rear of the vehicle. "Well?"

Opening the back door, Luca took out his sword and strapped it on. "I'll fight them. Keep them too busy to return to Chad and let him know where we are."

"No." She placed a hand on his forearm. "Why didn't you say? I thought we'd keep driving. How did you stay ahead of them last night? You said they can't go fast for long periods."

"I ran."

"Then do that tonight."

"I cannot carry you all night and remain ahead of them."

She hadn't realised it'd be so dangerous for him. Why hadn't he said something? An image came to her of Luca talking about the amount of times he'd been killed. "Leave me behind and go."

He ran his fingers lightly down her cheek. "Even if I could leave you unprotected, I wouldn't."

She didn't want him hurt because of her. "Luca–"

"There's time before they arrive. They have to travel from where I left them."

"Where was that?"

"South west of Brisbane. Which is why we travelled north." He took her hand. "Come for a walk along the water's edge with me."

"How will that help?"

"I want to show you the lay of the land."

"That sounds like something you'd say when planning for a battle." She tried to make out his expression, but the light from the moon didn't do much to help.

"When the demons find us stay near the ocean. The salt is diluted, but it'll cause them pain to enter the water. Not much, but maybe enough to make a difference." Bending, he unstrapped a sheathed dagger from his ankle, that was beneath the leg of his jeans, and held it out to her. "To protect yourself."

"I don't know how to use it."

"Holy water has been tipped over the blade. It'll not take much of a cut for a demon to feel the pain from this dagger."

"Why didn't you tell me how much danger it'd put you in if I came with you?"

"I'm not accustomed to that being an issue."

She'd been right. Not that being right made her happy to hear the matter of fact tone he used. Stepping close, she placed her hand against his chest. "It is an issue. And I want you to take it into account in future."

Luca inclined his head. "If you wish, my little ninja."

She momentarily felt his amusement. "I'm serious."

"I know. But you worry over nothing. I can't be killed." He stepped away from her, holding out his hand. "I've not yet finished showing you the area."

She took his hand, walking with him along the beach, glad of the pale expanse that stretched out in front of them making it easier to see in the limited light. "Where are we going?"

"There's an inlet in this direction. If for any reason you need to run, try and take the other direction. And don't go upstream if you should need to come this way. The salt becomes more diluted."

They stopped at where the water cut off one section of the beach from the other. Penelope stared at the darkness of the water. "So I don't go in this direction?"

"Or if you do, remain on the beach."

"Okay."

"If you go in the other direction, stay away from the tree line. There are rocks scattered across the beach above the high tide mark."

Her grip tightened on the dagger she continued to hold. "This doesn't seem like a good idea. Go without me."

"There's more in the world than demons. I'll not leave you unprotected." He took her hand again and walked with her back along the beach. Reaching the part of the beach in front of the vehicle, he gestured towards it. "Would you like a blanket to sit on?"

"No." She sat on the sand, wriggling until it shifted, creating a comfortable spot. "How long will they be?"

He sat beside her. "A few hours. Possibly longer. They can't travel at great speed for hours on end. They may even conserve their strength and go at a more normal pace when they realise we're stationary."

"I don't like waiting."

Luca chuckled. "Did you think you would get out of waiting by coming with me?"

"I guess." She leaned against him, smiling when he slid an arm around her. "Tell me some more about the places you've been." She closed her eyes, listening to the sound of his voice as he talked about places that no longer existed, ones he'd like to see again and those he thought she might enjoy. A slight smile remained in place as she listened, occasionally asking questions, wishing the night would never end and the demons wouldn't find them. When hours passed, she began to hope the demons weren't coming.

Luca stopped mid sentence. "They're close."

She pulled away from him, grabbing the dagger she'd placed beside her. "How close?"

Luca rose to his feet, holding out his hand. "Minutes away."

Fear shivered through her as she took his hand, continuing to clutch the dagger. "I don't think I can do this."

"You have more courage than you think."

She took a step away from him. "No. I don't."

Luca chuckled softly. "You do. And soon you'll know that too." He turned away from her. "It's less than two hours until sunrise. All we have to do is hold them off until then."

That didn't sound too bad. She changed her mind when she saw the demons come out of the tree line, headed for them. Even though there was very little light, she didn't need much to see how large the three demons were. "I thought you said there were only two."

"There were two last night." Luca drew his sword. "Chad must have called a third."

She removed the dagger from its sheath, tossing the sheath onto the sand. Before she could say anything, Luca rushed forward to attack the demon that tried to leave the area. He was a blur of motion, going from one demon to the next. Then he was stuck fighting two of the demons while the third managed to escape.

She tried not to think about what that meant. If he was going to bring Chad back, there wasn't a lot of time left before daylight. Remaining close to the water, she watched the fight, her grip on the dagger remaining tight. She wished there was more light. Only being able to hear the clash of metal, the demons wielding swords equally as fast as Luca, left her worried about what was happening.

As the night wore on, she began to realise exactly how long a couple of hours was. She wanted to help

Luca, not stand around feeling useless. Several times she checked her phone, willing the time to move faster. It didn't. The minutes ticked by and the battle continued. Several times a demon came close to her, but Luca got between her and the demon at the last second.

She was beginning to think everything would be fine. That the sun would rise and Chad wouldn't arrive before his demons vanished. Looking at the screen of her phone again she saw there was only twenty minutes until sunrise. Hope rose. They could manage this. A shot rang out and fear raced through her, blinking as she realised Luca was in front of her, staggering. For a split second she felt his pain.

"Luca?" Before she could reach for him, he was gone, rushing into the shadows of the tree line.

Two demons came towards her.

She clutched the dagger tightly, holding it in front of her. "I will use this."

One of the demons laughed. "Do you think that scares us?"

Several shots sounded from the tree line and she wanted to run towards Luca. Wanted to see that he was okay. "It should. It has holy water on it."

"You have to be able to cut us with it first." The demon leapt forward, knocking her off her feet.

She landed in the water, the dagger knocked from her hand, the sea dragging sand away from her back. Struggling against the demon's grip, she coughed and spluttered as a wave washed over her face.

"He doesn't care how you die, as long as you do." The demon dragged her further into the sea.

It was impossible to escape from the grip of the demon, but she fought against him anyway. Holding her breath, she hit out at him. Her efforts made no difference. He remained immoveable. When she tried to raise her head out of the water, he pushed her back under. Her lungs burned and she tried not to breathe, her hands hitting him ineffectually.

"Fighting is a waste of time."

It might have been, but she couldn't do anything else. Unable to hold her breath a moment longer, saltwater filled her lungs, burning, blackness rushing in on her.

Chapter Thirteen

"Penelope." There was fear in Luca's tone. "Penny! Speak to me."

She tried to move, wanting to reassure Luca, panicking when she realised her body was trapped. Breathing in, pain arrowed through her and she began coughing. The tightness around her reduced and she opened her eyes to see he held her. "What happened?" Her voice sounded raspy and her throat ached.

"You're alive."

She pulled away from him to sit up. "Of course I'm alive." She frowned as the night came back to her. There was a faint grey in the sky, heralding the arriving dawn. "Why am I alive?" She hadn't thought she'd survive. "And where are the demons? I thought they'd remain until sunrise."

"The deal Chad made with them meant they had to

return to where they came from once I was no longer bound to you."

Nothing made sense. "I'm no longer your master?"

"You're my master again."

"What happened, Luca?"

"You died."

The words rang in her head, making as little sense as they had when Luca had spoken them. "But I'm alive."

"I brought you back."

"How?" Her gaze narrowed.

Luca smiled fleetingly. "There was no magic involved. I resuscitated you."

She stood up, stumbling when her legs gave way. "I died."

He reached for her. "Yes."

She took a step away. "Why didn't you run? Why did you touch me?"

"Because you would now be dead."

"You could have been free."

"Would I? How free would you have been if you'd let me return to my previous master?"

"Oh." She twisted a lock of hair between her fingers, letting go the moment she realised what she was doing. She noticed the watch was on her wrist. "Why am I wearing this?"

"Because you haven't given me permission to touch it."

"Yes, I have. The first time I met you." She hadn't exactly given him permission, but he'd taken the indistinguishable sound she'd made as an agreement.

"All orders need to be given again. The bond was broken."

"All orders?" She couldn't remember exactly what orders she'd given him. "Can I say everything is to be the same as it was before?"

"That will work." He slid the watch off her wrist, undoing the catch so he could put it on his own.

Feeling uncomfortable to see him willingly take that which kept him cursed, forever a jinn, she looked away. She noticed Chad lying on the sand not far from the tree line. "He's dead?"

"No."

"Did you knock him out?"

"I rendered him unconscious."

"What's the difference?"

"One uses pressure points while the other uses force."

"How come he didn't end up being your master?"

"I let go of him a few seconds before you died. I ran towards you, but it was too late."

She eyed him, trying to figure out what was

wrong. "Are you okay?" She remembered all the shots that had been fired. "Did he shoot you?"

"I'll heal once the wounds are cleaned."

Reaching for him, she tried to lift up his shirt.

He captured her hand. "Later. We need to leave before Chad is conscious."

"What's wrong?"

"Do you not complain I ask that question too often?"

"Luca." Her throat ached when she raised her voice.

"Are you ordering me to tell you?"

For a moment she was tempted. Resignation struck. "No."

Luca drew her against him, holding her tight. It was several minutes before he spoke. "I felt you die. It isn't the first time I've felt a master die, but it's the first time I have cared."

"I'm sorry."

He drew back enough to meet her gaze. "What have you to be sorry for?"

"I should have fought harder."

"Against two demons? Did you really expect to win when you faced two demons, with no skill of your own, and a single dagger?"

She smiled. "No, but I fought anyway." Her smile

slowly faded. "It actually felt pretty good. Or it did until they drowned me."

His arms tightened around her. "Let us not speak of that moment for now."

"Okay." She'd rather not think of it either. "Can we go somewhere we can have a shower and get into dry clothes?" A pity she'd left the bag of clothes at Luca's house. She should have brought it with her.

"Yes." Luca gathered their weapons and walked back to the vehicle with his arm around her shoulders. When she was seated, he stared at her a moment longer before he closed the door.

She was tempted to ask him what he was thinking. But she feared it was something to do with her death. And she really didn't want to discuss that. Or think about it. She thought of Rusty. Would he have missed her if she'd died? After a moment she decided he would. After all, he'd returned to her. The only one who ever had.

They arrived in a nearby town and Luca found a motel for them to stay in. He paid someone to collect their clothes and take them away to be laundered. They wore the bathrobes Luca had arranged to be provided and Penelope smiled when Luca came out of the bathroom. Her robe fit far better than his.

"What amuses you?"

"A towel would cover more of you than that robe."

Luca chuckled. "And yours covers far too much."

She came forward, wrapping her arms around him. "I'll wait behind in future. Until we travel to the resting place of Solomon. Chad was nearly your master."

"It wasn't your fault."

"It feels like it."

"It was mine. I should have protected you better. I let my arrogance over never having lost a master allow you to be killed."

"I'm alive."

"But you were dead for a few seconds." His arms tightened around her.

"You could have left, but you didn't. You could have been free." She could barely believe he hadn't run.

"I never would have been free. Your death would have haunted me for the rest of my life."

"Really?" She drew back so she could see his expression, annoyed to find it guarded. Before she could say anything, his feelings washed over her, the same ones as previously, this time more intense. "That's a very handy trick. Better than simple words."

"Words are good too."

Before she could speak any words, his lips met hers

and she returned the kiss, her arms tightening around him. They remained wrapped in each other's arms until there was a knock on the door. She drew away to stare at it, fear racing through her.

"It will be breakfast."

"Oh." The fear remained, her heart beating too fast. She stayed behind Luca as he opened the door and took the food. The fear didn't start to fade until the door was closed again.

They ate silently and when they were finished, Penelope used Luca's phone to ring the priest since hers no longer worked after being soaked by seawater. She'd been surprised to find he'd put the priest's number into his contact list. Listening to the phone ring, she hoped the priest didn't like to sleep in.

"Father Joe."

She was relieved he sounded awake. "It's Penelope. I was wondering if Emily and Dan have returned."

"I'm afraid they still can't be contacted. Is there something I can help you with?"

"No, but I need to give you a different number as my phone was damaged." She waited for him to find pen and paper before she rattled it off.

"Are you certain there's nothing I can help you with?"

"No. I really need to talk to Emily." She tried to keep the desperation from her voice, certain she'd failed. "Thanks anyway. Bye." She hung up before he could ask her once more, turning to Luca. "What are we going to do? Can you find them? You know, like the demons can find you."

He shook his head. "Demons track people by using their blood. I don't have that ability. The only one I can find is you, through our bond."

The phone beeped and she automatically checked the message, her jaw dropping when she read what the priest had sent. *Does your problem involve demons?*

Luca took the phone from her. "He knows."

"Why didn't he say something earlier?"

"I cannot imagine many people would be willing to admit to knowing about demons. Humans think them a myth." He held the phone out to her. "Do you wish to ring him?"

Her legs felt weak and her head light. She stumbled to the small table they'd eaten breakfast at, nearly missing the chair when she tried to sit down. "What would I say to him?"

"That you need help. That demons wish to kill you and you need to break the curse of a jinn so they'll stop hunting you."

She had the urge to laugh, then wondered if that

was what hysteria felt like. "What if…" Her words trailed off. What if he didn't believe her? She couldn't think of a single person who'd believe anything that had happened to her recently.

Luca crouched in front of her, looking up to meet her gaze. "What is wrong?"

His familiar words brought a smile to her lips and some of the panic receded. Reaching for him, she wrapped her arms around him, his head pressed against her chest, her head resting on his. "Don't you get sick of asking me that?"

"I will always want to know if something is wrong. I'd rather you told me, but if you don't I'll always ask." He drew back to meet her gaze.

She nearly asked him how long was always. Until he returned to his family's home? Longer? Her courage failed. Fighting demons was easier than asking that question. Which was sad considering she had no idea how to fight and the only time she'd fought them she'd ended up dead.

"Penny?"

"You called me that earlier." She'd forgotten. There'd been other things to worry about.

"Does it bother you?"

It took her a moment to answer. "Not the way you say it." With his accent it didn't sound common like her grandmother had told her it was when she'd let a friend call her that years ago.

"I assume there's a story involving inappropriateness."

Laughter burst from her, startling her. "Isn't there always?"

"Not in the future."

She was glad she was sitting when she felt a fierce protective feeling wash over her. "You can't stop it."

"You can. You'll do what you desire regardless of inappropriateness according to your family. Their definition of the word is shallow."

"Possibly."

"You died this morning. What if I'd not been able to resuscitate you? Have you lived the life you wanted?"

She could only shake her head, remembering the pain of saltwater rushing into her lungs as she took an overdue breath.

"Next time they tell you something is inappropriate, remember that moment."

"Okay."

"You don't sound convincing."

A rush of memories crowded in on her. The earlier ones filled with joy, the later ones filled with worry and denial. "My life didn't flash before my eyes. Isn't it meant to do that when you die?"

"Not always."

She started to ask him how he knew. "Oh." He'd had hundreds of more experience than her when it came to dying.

Luca held out his phone. "Do you wish to call the priest or should I?"

Chapter Fourteen

Penelope stared at the phone for a moment before she reached for it, closing her hand over the phone, not taking it from Luca. "I'll ring."

"That's the conviction I was looking for earlier."

She held his gaze with her own, not flinching from the intensity. "I will live my life." She took the phone from him, rising to her feet so he was forced to do the same. She was sick of letting other people live it for her.

"Good."

She smiled when he let his feelings wash over her. It was good. Now if only she could hold onto her conviction the next time she faced down her mother. Or her grandmother. Pushing aside those worries, she called the priest.

"Father Joe."

"It's Penelope."

"Can I help you, Penelope?"

"I don't know."

"Did you receive my text?"

"Yes."

"Is that why you're calling?"

It took her a moment to bring herself to answer him. A moment to remind herself that he wouldn't think her crazy. He was the one who'd mentioned demons first. "A man wants me dead because I have something he wants and he's called demons to make sure I die. Again."

There was a moment of silence before Father Joe spoke. "Again."

She hesitated once more. When Luca stepped close, she took hold of his hand, meeting his gaze. "It was only for a few seconds. My…" She stumbled over her words, having nearly said 'boyfriend'. Her gaze was drawn to her hand in Luca's. "A jinn resuscitated me. I need to break his curse. I don't want to be his master." Her voice broke on the last word. She wanted to be something far different to that. When Luca's hand tightened on hers, she met his gaze, surprised to see he was smiling.

"I'll give you an address."

"I don't have pen or paper."

"I'll text it to you. Let me know when you can get there and I'll have hunters organised to talk to you."

"Hunters?" Hadn't he said Emily and Dan couldn't be contacted?

"Demon hunters. I come from an entire family of hunters. They'll help you."

That sounded exactly like what she needed. What they both needed. "Thank you."

"You're not alone. We can help you."

She blinked back the tears that wanted to fall. "Thank you. I really need to set him free." She should be happy, not wanting to burst into tears.

"Of course you do. I'll send you that text now and you call me back if you have any problems."

Again she thanked him before hanging up, throwing her arms around Luca. "We're going to set you free. You'll be able to go home." She tried to focus on the happiness she should be feeling for him.

"Home is closer than I thought."

Before she could ask him what he meant, a text message came through. Checking, she saw it was the address. "We have to return to Brisbane."

Luca took the phone from her. "As soon as our clothes are ready. Have a rest while we wait. I'll let the priest know when we're likely to arrive."

They didn't leave the moment the clothes were

ready. Luca insisted on getting a replacement phone for Penelope and she was relieved when her sim card worked in the new phone. Her relief evaporated when she realised there was nothing on the card that was important to her apart from a single phone number. None of the photos and none of the numerous numbers in her contact list. How had she reached this point? An image of Suzie and Harrison wrapped in each other's arms came to her. The appropriate boyfriend and appropriate friend. So much for how appropriate they'd both been.

"What is wrong?"

Taking his hand, she threaded her fingers through his. "I actually think something is right."

"I felt your pain."

"Yes, but it was the good sort of pain."

"What type of pain is good?"

"The one that keeps you from making the same mistake over and over again." She was obviously a slow learner. And Luca was wrong. It wasn't her death she needed to remember next time she was told something was appropriate for her. Or inappropriate. It was the appropriate things that hadn't been right for her. "Let's go. We have some demon hunters to meet and a curse to break." Her enthusiasm lasted less than twenty minutes. The amount of time it took to fall asleep in the vehicle, the seat having been covered by towels to soak up the water from earlier.

"Penny?"

She blinked, trying to bring Luca's face into focus. Realising it was late afternoon she looked out the window. "We're here?" They were parked in front of a spacious timber house beside a dark coloured all wheel drive. The house was painted in neutral creams and browns and nestled amongst flowering gardens. "Are you sure this is the right place?" It looked normal. Not like a place to meet demon hunters.

"What were you expecting? A castle?"

"No, but something that looks a little more secure. This place looks like anyone could break in. Even a demon." It'd be a long time before she forgot how strong demons were.

"It will be sacred ground. Like the graveyard."

"People are buried here?"

Luca chuckled. "No. It only needs to be blessed."

"Oh." She started to reach for a strand of her hair, lowering her hand when she realised what she was doing.

"Are you ready to go inside?"

Not in the slightest. "Yeah."

He clasped her hand between both of his. "I'll remain at your side."

She met his gaze, unable to ask him how long he would do that for. "Will demons be able to find us here once it's dark?"

"Yes."

"Then let's get on with it so we can be out of here before then. I don't want to bring demons to their door. That seems like a really terrible way to repay someone who's going to help us." She reluctantly drew her hand from between his, clambering out of the vehicle.

Reaching the front door, she stared at it, taking almost a minute to be able to knock on the timber. The young man who opened it had dark eyes that were nearly black, an angular face with slashing cheeks, close cropped dark hair, broad shoulders, a row of earrings up both ears and in one eyebrow and her family would have thought him thoroughly inappropriate. In his black jeans and t-shirt he looked exactly like what she needed.

"You must be Penelope." He held out his hand. "I'm Jesse."

She shook his hand. "I'm Penelope."

Jesse turned to Luca. "And you're definitely a jinn." He held out his hand.

Luca took it, frowning. "You are some kind of demon?"

A young woman joined Jesse, brown eyes narrowed as she hit his arm with the back of her hand. "Stop doing that. One day you'll go too far and become a demon again." Her short blond hair feathered around her fine boned face and she had a small gold cross on a cord necklace around her throat. Like Jesse, she was also dressed in black.

Jesse grinned. "I'd never risk being unable to be at your side, Lady Knight."

Slowly shaking her head, she turned to Penelope and Luca. "Come inside. Father Joe said you want to break a curse. I'm Scarlett Hunter."

Nodding, Penelope followed Scarlett, leaving her shoes with the ones near the front door. She stopped in the doorway of a room to the right of the front door. It was a spacious lounge room with a pale brown lounge suite set around a rustic coffee table and a couple of large square footstools. There were groups of pictures hung on the wall, a long display cabinet filled with ornaments along one of the walls and the wall opposite the door was taken up by a floor to ceiling built-in bookcase with glass doors. Afternoon light entered the room from a large window to her right.

A young man rose from an armchair. He had a square jaw, sharp cheekbones, deep brown eyes, a solemn look and broad shoulders. Coming forward, he held out his hand. "I'm Alex Hunter."

Penelope automatically moved forward to take his hand. She looked from Alex to Scarlett. "You're related?" She frowned. "I thought the priest said you were demon hunters. He didn't say anything about your surnames being Hunter."

Alex smiled fleetingly. "We're siblings. We hear that a lot. Our family have been hunting demons for centuries." He nodded towards Luca. "Ask your jinn. People were once named for their occupations."

Scarlett gestured towards the lounge suite. "Take a seat and tell us exactly what the problem is."

Penelope stared at Scarlett's left wrist. A thin black line went around her wrist nearly three times. "What does the tattoo mean?" She looked to Alex and Jesse, noticing they had them too. Jesse also had a tattoo of a black feather on his left palm.

"They aren't tattoos. They're demon marks and gained from dealing with demons." Scarlett sat in one of the armchairs, Jesse sitting on the arm of her chair.

When Alex returned to sitting in the other armchair, Penelope sat in the double seater, relieved Luca would be able to sit beside her. She hadn't expected three hunters or that they'd all be around her age. Her gaze was drawn to Jesse. Although it was possible he was a lot older since he'd once been a demon. She had no idea how that worked, but had too many of her own problems to worry about it for more than a few seconds.

Luca took hold of Penelope's hand, his gaze on the hunters. "I need the help of a virgin over the age of consent to help break my curse. They would need to be willing to travel with us to the resting place of Solomon."

When Scarlett began to speak, Jesse interrupted her. "I wouldn't be able to travel there without becoming a demon again."

"You don't have to go everywhere with me," Scarlett said.

Jesse smiled and lifted her hand to his lips in answer.

Scarlett returned his smile before facing Penelope. "I'm sorry. I can't help you. But I'm not the only hunter. One of us will be able to help." Her gaze travelled to Luca. "No one should be trapped a slave no matter what they've done."

Luca spoke before Penelope could voice her surprise at Scarlett being a virgin. "Are you asking me to tell you the story?"

Scarlett shook her head. "As much as I'd like to hear it, that's up to you. It won't change anything. We'll help regardless."

"I'm willing to tell you the tale, but it would take more than a few minutes and sunset is drawing closer. We didn't want to bring demons to your doorstep."

Jesse chuckled. "They know of this house. Very few risk coming here."

"There are humans involved. Ones who are willing to kill all who stand in their way of regaining control of me," Luca said.

"You can tell us later," Scarlett said.

"Does the virgin have to be female?" Alex spoke to Luca. "Is it gender related?"

"It wasn't specified when the curse was created."

Penelope stared open mouthed at Alex. Both him and his sister? That didn't seem possible. "You're a virgin?"

Alex turned his gaze to her. "I don't condemn your beliefs, have the courtesy not to mock mine when we're trying to help you."

"But..." Her voice trailed off as she realised telling him he was too gorgeous to be a virgin would probably be as bad as the other comment she'd blurted out. "Sorry. I wasn't mocking. You surprised me." They both had.

"Are you willing to give it a go?" Scarlett asked Alex.

"It'll be dangerous. We'll need to travel through the home of the jinni to reach the resting place of Solomon. They'll not willingly let us through if we should come across any of them," Luca warned.

"We could ask others to help," Scarlett said.

"What about Emily and Dan?" Penelope asked.

Scarlett shook her head. "We don't know when they'll be back. They're following up on one of her premonitions. Emily didn't think you'd get in touch. She mentioned meeting you when her and Dan called in to see Riley. We have no way to contact them."

"It's a pity Riley went with them," Alex said. "We could ask Gabe."

Again Scarlett shook her head. "Remedy would never let Cassidy go where he couldn't and she wouldn't want Gabe to go without her. Besides, I don't think it's a good place for them to be."

Chapter Fifteen

Penelope began to fear the demon hunters wouldn't be able to help.

"They could go with us to the entrance," Jessie said.

"Us?" Scarlett smiled up at him.

"I know you want to protect your brother, Lady Knight. To the entrance only. Not beyond," Jesse said.

"What about Malachi? He's back in town," Alex said.

Scarlett slowly nodded. "Yes. He'd be perfect." She rose to her feet. "I'll call him." She turned to her brother. "You call Gabe and Cassidy and ask them if they can go with us to the entrance." She turned to Luca. "Where is the entrance?"

"In the depths of the earth."

"Where exactly?" Scarlett asked.

"There is no actual location. One must enter the

earth through a cave or tunnel, man made or natural, and ask permission of the jinni to let them in," Luca said.

"What if they refuse?" Jesse asked.

Luca grinned. "They would never refuse one of their own." His grin faded. "One of you they'd refuse. Especially you with your occasional faint scent of demon, but never their own. No matter what one of us has done we're always allowed home. But it doesn't mean the reception will be friendly."

"How long will it take to travel through the home of the jinni to the resting place of Solomon?" Alex asked.

Luca shrugged. "Hours. Days. Months. It'll depend on what we face and how well we face it."

Alex rose from the chair. "I'll pack enough supplies for a week."

"Confidence or arrogance?" Luca asked.

Alex grinned fleetingly. "Neither. Any more and I'd slow myself down with too much gear."

Luca inclined his head. "I'll organise what we need. May I leave Penelope in your care while I prepare?"

"I can go with you." She didn't want to be left with strangers.

"I'll be able to gather what we need far quicker if I go alone."

She wanted to protest, but thoughts of the last time she'd demanded to go with him were too vivid. "Okay."

Luca drew her close, holding both her hands. "You'll be safe here."

When she would have moved closer and kissed him, he stepped away. About to protest, she stopped when a rush of feelings washed over her. Before she had a chance to do the same, he was gone. It didn't matter. He could sense how she felt no matter where he was. She let him feel her emotions. The worry, the fear and most of all the fierce protective feeling she had for him. Her love for him threaded through it. Her breath caught in her throat. Love. That wasn't meant to happen. She'd met him Saturday night and it was only Tuesday. Not even night yet.

"Are you okay?" Jesse asked.

She faced him, the similarity of the words continuing to make her think of Luca. "Yes."

"Are you sure?"

She glanced around the room. "Where are Scarlett and Alex?"

"Calling for reinforcements and getting ready. Are you sure you're okay?"

"Of course I am."

"I hope so. Because if something goes wrong and Alex gets hurt Scarlett will be devastated."

She was tempted to ask him if he was threatening her. "I'm okay and nothing is going to go wrong." She tried not to think about dying that morning.

"Good." Jesse paused a moment. "Can you fight?"

She shook her head.

"Then make sure you stay out of the way."

Annoyance rose and she barely managed not to curl her hand into a fist. "I'm not going to get anyone hurt." Her phone beeped and she checked the message, smiling when she saw it was from Luca, her annoyance fading.

What is wrong?

Still smiling, she answered him. *I miss you.*

That does not answer the question, but I will be back shortly and you can tell me then.

About to put her phone away, she decided to message her mother first. After letting her know they were going into poor mobile phone coverage areas and that she'd text if she had coverage, she returned her phone to her pocket.

Jesse nodded to where she'd put her phone. "Any problems?"

"No." When Jesse continued to examine her, she demanded, "What is your problem?'

"I can't help feeling you're hiding something."

She reached for a strand of her hair, stopping at the last second. For a moment she was tempted to tell him that she hid nothing. "I should have talked to Emily Sunday morning. But I didn't."

"You wanted your own jinn to order around?"

"Not exactly." Again she fought the urge to twist a strand of hair between her fingers.

"Power?"

"No." Her gaze was drawn to her bare feet. "I wanted something that couldn't be taken from me."

"If something can be taken from you then it wasn't worth having or you didn't fight hard enough for it. Or try and get it back."

She met his gaze. "It's not always that easy."

"I didn't say it was easy."

She opened her mouth then closed it again. No, he hadn't said it was easy. A smile slowly formed. "I guess you didn't."

Jesse grinned. "No more easy path?"

She thought of Rusty. There was no way she was going to let him be taken from her again. She tried not to think of Luca. He needed to return home. She couldn't be cruel enough to stop him from doing that. "I think the path is going to become more than a little rocky in the future."

Jesse nodded. "Good. And make sure you stay out of the way. If you don't know how to fight you'll only cause problems." He held up a hand when she started to protest. "It's advice, not an insult."

"Okay."

Alex entered the lounge room, a backpack slung over one shoulder, a sheathed sword in one hand. "Everyone will be here soon. How long until Luca returns?"

She couldn't drag her gaze from the sword. "I don't know."

"Did he tell you where we need to go to enter the home of the jinni?" Alex asked.

Penelope finally managed to drag her gaze from the sword. "No."

There was a knock on the door. Before anyone could move, Scarlett called out from the foyer, "I've got it." A few seconds later she entered the room, followed by Luca and a young man dressed in black, his dark hair tied back in a pony tail at the nape of his neck.

He had two sheathed swords with him, holding them in his right hand as he glanced around the room. His gaze stopped on Penelope. "You must be the one who owns the jinn." He grinned, nodding towards Luca when he said the word 'jinn'. "I'm

Malachi." He transferred his swords to his left hand, holding out his right.

She took his hand, having noticed his demon mark went around his wrist four times. "Thanks for helping."

Malachi shrugged. "It beats the other plans I had for the night."

"What were they?" She glanced at Luca who came to stand by her side.

"I'm on call for clean up duty this month."

"Clean up duty?"

Malachi chuckled. "Yeah, demons tend to leave a mess. Someone has to deal with it otherwise there'd be a lot of unexplainable questions. Particularly from the police."

"Oh."

Two more entered the room, causing Luca to step in front of Penelope. "You invited demons?"

"No." Scarlett came forward. "They're tainted. Not demons." She gestured to each of them in turn. "Cassidy and Gabe. They'll come to the entrance with us."

Both were dressed in black, neither appearing to carry any weapons with them. Penelope hoped that didn't mean they were unarmed. After her encounter with the demons she had to think it'd be a very bad idea to face them without a single weapon. "Can we leave now? Demons will be after us once it's dark." She glanced towards the window, trying not to think of how little light was left of the day.

"Where are we going?" Jesse asked.

"An abandoned mine," Luca said.

"How do you know it'll be suitable?" Scarlett asked.

"Because I was there when it was started and there when it closed. I made certain I'd be able to enter it again if I ever needed to," Luca said.

"How far away is it?" Jesse asked.

"A couple of hours north."

Luca's words made fear race through Penelope. North made her think of demons, the beach and dying.

Malachi looked to Penelope. "Alex and I will go with you two. The rest of my gear is in the foyer."

It didn't take long for all of them to gather their gear, put on shoes and head outside. Scarlett and Jesse took the all wheel drive while Cassidy and Gabe got on a motorbike, Cassidy in front. They followed behind Luca's four-wheel-drive as he pulled out onto the street and headed north.

"How did you end up with a jinn?"

Penelope turned in her seat so she could look at Malachi. "It was an accident."

"Does that mean it's none of our business?" Malachi asked.

"No." She couldn't exactly refuse since they were putting their lives at risk to help her.

Luca glanced in the rear view mirror. "My previous master was clinically dead for a few minutes. I escaped while they revived him. Penelope had the misfortune to touch me when I was without a master."

She wouldn't exactly call it a misfortune, not now. "I ran into him with my car."

Malachi chuckled. "Glad you're not the one driving."

"There's nothing wrong with how I drive. Luca stepped out in front of me." She glared at Malachi.

"You could always start from the beginning of the story and then Malachi wouldn't need to jump to conclusions," Alex suggested.

"It's Luca's story," Penelope said.

"I'll tell it if you wish to hear," Luca said.

Malachi shrugged. "Not much else to do on a long drive other than talk."

While darkness fell, Penelope listened as Luca retold his story, noticing he kept the details more brief than he had for her. Sensing hastily masked feelings, she reached out and rested a hand on his thigh, wanting him to know he wasn't alone. Not anymore. He momentarily covered her hand with his before returning it to the steering wheel. Luca finished the story with an accounting of the morning's events. Including Penelope's death.

Malachi and Alex asked a few questions, mostly Malachi, and eventually they all fell silent. Luca turned off the highway about an hour and a half from when they'd left the hunter's house and travelled along roads that began to slowly deteriorate until they were on a narrow dirt road filled with ruts and overgrown with grass and small shrubs in places.

"Are we nearly there?" Penelope held onto the handle in the roof above the window, bracing herself against the jarring drive.

"Soon."

"How soon? And if this road leads all the way there, how come no one else has found it?" Penelope asked.

"The road ends before we reach the abandoned mine."

"Clean up duty is starting to look a lot better," Malachi muttered.

Alex chuckled. "You'll change your mind once we're fighting."

"A warning that we'd have to traipse through the bush would have been good," Malachi said.

Penelope agreed with him. "I've never been bushwalking before."

Luca momentarily rested his hand on Penelope's leg. "It's only a short walk."

His words didn't make her feel any better. Not when she looked out her window at the darkness that surrounded them. Anything could be out there. Besides the demons that were coming after them.

The road ended abruptly, large gum trees blocking their way. Luca stopped the vehicle and turned off the engine. The lights went out, only the ones from the vehicles behind keeping the darkness at bay.

Malachi turned on a torch he took from the backpack at his feet. "I can feel demons coming in fast."

Luca swung the door open. "They would have summoned more. The ones that were after us have finished their terms of service." He went around to the back of the vehicle and took out his sword, strapping it on before he pulled out a backpack and slung it into place.

Chapter Sixteen

Penelope followed Malachi to the back of the vehicle to speak to Luca, glad for the light from the torch. "Why aren't the other three demons coming after us?"

"When you died their contract ended. We were no longer bound." Luca closed the back of the vehicle.

"Oh."

Alex joined them at the same time as the lights of the other vehicles were turned off. He held a torch. "The demons are likely to reach us before we reach the mine. Unless it's only a few minutes away."

Scarlett walked towards them, carrying a lantern. "It doesn't matter. We'll send them back to hell while you lot escape."

Cassidy followed Scarlett, holding Gabe's hand, neither of them carrying either torches or lanterns. "People never learn demons shouldn't be messed with. They're not minions suitable for doing your dirty work."

"Maybe you should remember that," Scarlett said to Cassidy.

Gabe laughed. "There are always exceptions to the rule."

Penelope looked at each of them, not sure she wanted to know what they were talking about. "Are we heading to the mine now?"

Luca shook his head. "We'll wait for the demons. There's a clearing a little way in. The mine is directly west of the clearing. If the demons don't know where we are, neither will Eugene or Chad. We have to return here when we come back."

"Oh." She hadn't known that.

"They'll know where your vehicle is," Gabe said.

"Better than if they waited at the mine exit, keeping us from escaping," Luca said.

Penelope didn't like either option. Before she could say so, Scarlett spoke.

"Lead the way. It'd be good to have a few minutes to check out the lay of the land."

Penelope looked from Luca to Scarlett, surprised the hunter used the same words Luca had used yesterday when preparing for battle. She found them reassuring. Following Luca as he threaded his way through the trees, she began to feel less worried about the arriving demons. They might actually survive. She forced away memories of that morning.

When they stepped into the clearing, the hunters paced the area, Scarlett placing her lantern behind them on the ground. They faced the direction the demons would come from, Cassidy played with a small dagger she'd drawn from under her shirt. Gabe stood beside her, no weapons visible, while the rest held their swords, Malachi holding two that were shorter than the ones Alex and Scarlett held. Penelope wondered what had happened to the dagger Luca had given her yesterday and why he hadn't given her one tonight. Before she could ask, three demons burst into the clearing, the scent of sulphur and charcoal filling the air around them.

"A forth demon fled before it could reach us," Luca warned.

"We noticed," Gabe said.

Penelope hadn't and as much as she wanted to ask them how they knew, she remained silent, her gaze fixed on the creatures in front of her. The one in the middle had scaly, greenish skin, wings rising behind him. He formed a sword from the air, a dark blade that seemed like it had been created from the night. She took a step back, fighting the urge to run.

Reassurance washed over her and she looked towards Luca who faced the demons.

As a group, the demons raced forward, the ones flanking the middle one calling their own swords from the air. No one spoke, only attacked. Gabe threw daggers at the demons. They hissed in pain when they were struck. He used the same type of dagger Cassidy had been playing with and now threw at a demon, drawing another one.

Penelope retreated a little further, her jaw dropping as she watched Cassidy and Gabe moving impossibly fast. Not as fast as Luca and the demons, but faster than it should have been possible for a human to move.

"We've got this if you want to go," Scarlett said. "We'll keep them from following you."

"They'll have a direction," Luca said.

"They have an area. They could use demons to search for the path you took," Gabe said.

"Or tracking dogs." Cassidy threw a dagger at the demon Scarlett fought. "I should have brought my sword. It's more fun than daggers." She threw another dagger, the demon snarling when it struck his body.

"Go," Scarlett ordered. "Before the other demon brings humans."

"Lead the way." Malachi dropped back, Gabe stepping in front of him.

Cassidy did the same for Alex, glancing at Gabe. "I told you I should have brought my sword." She withdrew two slightly longer daggers than the ones she'd been using and leapt forward, striking out at the demon before she catapulted over him.

Penelope froze, staring at Cassidy as she fought the demon, his attacks not managing to get anywhere near her. The hunter wouldn't have allowed two demons to drown her in shallow water.

Luca grabbed Penelope's upper arm. "There's no time to be entertained by the fight."

Penelope lengthened her stride to keep up with him. "Did you see Cassidy? It was like watching an action movie."

"When she first came to us she knew nothing about demons and not much about fighting." Alex shone his torch on the ground ahead of them.

"What changed?" Penelope asked.

"She learned," Alex said.

"Amongst other things." Malachi continued to hold one of his swords, a torch in the other hand.

She glanced at each of them, stumbling on a rock hidden by leaf litter. "That's it? She learned how to fight?"

Malachi chuckled. "Part of it. We all had to learn at some stage."

She stumbled again when she looked at Malachi as he spoke. This time she nearly went down.

Luca grabbed hold of her arm, keeping her on her feet. "Am I going too fast?"

She shook her head. "How much further?"

"We are close." Luca let go of her arm.

Malachi glanced around. "Everything looks the same to me."

"There are some differences," Alex said.

"Maybe to people who like camping. Not to those of us who try and avoid it like the plague." Malachi momentarily shone his torch ahead before returning the light to the ground in front. "It looks like we could walk for days and never find civilisation."

"That wouldn't surprise me," Alex said.

It wouldn't have surprised Penelope either. She moved closer to Luca, not wanting to get lost and test Malachi's theory.

A few minutes later Luca stopped near a lightning struck tree standing near dense scrub. He pushed branches aside, creeper vines tangling them together.

"Is it too overgrown to continue?" Malachi asked.

"We've arrived."

"This is a mine?" Penelope stared at the dense scrub

lit by the two torches. "How are we meant to get in there?"

"Carefully. If we tear the vines away it'll be easy to see where we went." Luca continued to work at the plants, separating them enough to show timber.

"There's a door." She'd had no idea what to expect, but it certainly hadn't been a door.

"To keep others from entering." Luca drew a large, old key from a pocket and inserted it into a lock he'd cleared the greenery from.

"Is that the way mines are usually closed?" Penelope watched Luca slowly open the door, brushing dirt and stones away from the base with his boot.

"They told me to seal it. This is how I closed it in the hope I could access it again later." Luca held the door, stepping back. "There should be enough space for all of us to enter."

Penelope took a step back. "Anything could be in there. Snakes, spiders, anything."

Malachi clapped Alex on the back. "Looks like you're going first. Didn't you say you liked camping?"

"This isn't camping." Alex gestured towards the opening with his torch, stepping forward.

Penelope was relieved. There was no way she wanted to go first. She followed behind Alex, trying not to think about what might be in the darkness ahead of them. When Alex stopped to brush his hand through spider webs, she took a step backwards, stumbling into Malachi. "Sorry."

"I noticed no one mentioned this part of the trip," Malachi said mildly.

Alex started to move forward again, his steps slow. "You didn't ask for details after we told you the destination."

"I guess that'll teach me," Malachi muttered. When Alex glanced over his shoulder at him, Malachi chuckled. "Okay, it probably won't."

A noise behind them had Penelope stopping to peer past Malachi, relieved he shone his torch in that direction.

Luca pulled the door closed behind him, locking it and pocketing the key as he faced them. "We need to travel deep into the earth before I can request entrance to the home of the jinni." He strode past all of them, taking the lead.

"How far is that?" Penelope noticed the ground sloped down slightly.

"There'll be no need to go down any of the shafts. The main tunnel will take us down far enough."

"Well that's a relief," Malachi said. "Abseiling into a dark pit sounds like a really bad idea. Even to me."

None of this sounded like a good idea to Penelope. Other than breaking the curse. She followed behind Luca and Alex, wishing it was Luca who carried the torch so she could walk closer to him. She didn't know the other two. Didn't trust that they'd be there for her like Luca would.

They remained silent. The only sounds were that of their boots against the rock and the occasional loose pebble skittering ahead of them. It felt like they'd been walking for hours, but when Penelope checked her phone it was to find only twenty minutes had passed. The slope of the tunnel had grown steeper and the loose pebbles and stones beneath their feet more noticeable.

Luca glanced over his shoulder. "We're nearly there."

She'd expected to be glad to hear those words, but if anything they left her with a sense of dread. What would the home of the jinni be like? Other than dangerous. Could you get more dangerous than being drowned by demons? A shiver ran through her as she remembered the water burning down her throat, filling her lungs.

Luca looked over his shoulder towards her. "Penelope?"

She tried to send him a feeling of reassurance.

Luca smiled. "You'll have to try better than that if you want me to believe."

"Am I missing something important?" Malachi looked from one to the other.

Penelope shook her head. "It's a jinni, master thing."

"You're worried." Alex spoke again once she nodded. "I didn't come along just to break the curse. I came to protect you too."

"Why?" When he didn't answer straight away, Penelope said, "You don't know me. I'm a stranger."

"It's our job," Malachi said. "Protecting humans from demons is what we're raised to do."

"That must be nice, knowing what you're going to do with your life." She couldn't keep the wistfulness from her tone. Not that it really mattered. She didn't have to hide how she felt from them. She doubted they'd go running to her parents with tales of inappropriateness.

"It's not something we're encouraged to do. We're taught to protect ourselves from demons and after that it's up to us if we want to become a hunter," Alex said.

"We've arrived." Luca faced a rough stone wall.

Alex stopped beside him, shining the torch up and down the wall.

"Here?" Penelope stepped to the other side of Luca. She'd expected another door.

Luca nodded, raising his hand to knock five times on the rock. "Exalted brother, I request entrance into the home of our kind."

"Who are you talking to?" Penelope had no idea why she whispered the words.

"Why did you knock five times?" Malachi asked.

"I am talking to one of the guards at the entrance of the home of the jinni. Five knocks are needed. One for each class of jinni."

Chapter Seventeen

Before Penelope could ask Luca what he meant, the wall in front of them sank back, forming a dark tunnel. "What is going on?"

"Humans?" A tall man walked towards them, stopping at the entrance of the dark tunnel. "You would bring humans into our home?" He faced Luca.

"Would you deny me entrance to the home of the jinni? Where all jinn are meant to be welcome."

The man gestured to Luca's companions. "These are not jinni. Humans are never welcome."

"They are my companions," Luca said.

"They are less than nothing." The guard's tone was filled with contempt. "They would control all of us if we allowed it." His lips curved into a mirthless smile and his eyes glittered with malice. "I have shown them the error of their ways thousands of times and

I am sure it will be necessary to do so a thousand more."

"Will you step aside so we can enter?" Luca asked.

"Will you bring the humans with you?" the guard demanded.

"If the jinni leave us alone, we'll leave them alone," Alex said.

The guard's eyes narrowed when he looked first at Alex, then Malachi, then Penelope. His gaze returned to Luca. "You brought two demon hunters with you?"

"We are passing through. We have no plans to stay."

"Where are you going?"

Luca didn't answer immediately. "The resting place of Solomon."

The guard stared at him for a moment before he threw back his head and laughed, the sound echoing off the rock walls around them.

Penelope wanted to demand what was so funny. She remained silent, doubting the guard would answer her with how little he thought of humans.

"Will you let us pass?" Luca asked again.

The guard's laughter trailed off, a grin remaining. "You do know what you have to face there."

Luca inclined his head.

Penelope once again remained silent when she would have preferred to ask a question. What would they face? What hadn't Luca told them?

The guard turned sideways, gesturing broadly for them to pass. "Then by all means, rush towards your death."

Penelope stayed close to Luca and tried to stay as far as possible from the guard as they entered the tunnel. Her fingers twisted at a strand of her hair and she didn't bother to let it go. Behind her she heard the hunters following, their light casting shadows ahead of her. The sound of rocks moving had her looking over her shoulder, her mouth gaping when she saw the tunnel close. How were they meant to escape?

"Penelope?"

She blinked, looking at Alex. "Yes?" Her voice was higher pitched than usual.

Before Alex could speak, Luca did, taking Penelope by the arm. "We need to keep moving. We have a lot of ground to cross." He looked past her to the guard, who stood behind Malachi, his arms crossed as he watched them.

Not wanting to be anywhere near the guard, Penelope nodded, turning in the direction they needed to go. She almost protested when Luca let go of her arm to walk ahead. She hurried after him, hearing the hunters' footsteps behind her, grateful for the light from their torches.

The tunnel was far longer than she'd expected. The composition of it changed, first the ground and then the walls and ceiling. The greyish stone was replaced by sandstone, loose grains of sand blowing across the ground as they neared the entrance, bright daylight casting an elongated circle on the floor. They paused in the entrance, looking out over the valley below them, the same grains of sand gusting across the ground in front of a city that appeared to be made from the sandstone mountains that encircled it. The mountain peaks reached into the harsh blue sky, towering over everything.

"Let me guess," Malachi said from behind Penelope. "We need to enter that city."

She looked over her shoulder, relieved to see only the two hunters were with them. The guard was nowhere to be seen. She faced Luca. "Surely we aren't going in there." Before they could cross the valley they'd need to climb down from the cave, which was halfway up the sandstone mountains.

"We'll not be strolling in the front gate."

Luca's words had Penelope looking towards the front gate, the people strolling through it looking tiny from this distance. "Are they all jinni?" She gestured towards the figures.

"I'd be surprised if they were anything else." Luca held out his hand to her. "Don't worry. I'll protect you."

"We'll all protect you," Alex said.

Penelope didn't take Luca's hand. "I'm not armed."

Luca lowered his hand before removing the sheathed dagger that was strapped to his calf beneath the leg of his jeans. He held it out to her.

Even though she had no idea how to use it, she took it from him, using the straps to attach it to a belt loop on her jeans. It hung awkwardly at her side, making her feel a little better about going to the city. Which was ridiculous. Even her grandmother would have thought it ridiculous. Something she couldn't use would be of no use to her.

"Are you ready?" Luca held out his hand again.

She was half tempted to say no. She placed her hand on his, surprised at how comforting it was when his fingers wrapped around hers. They were in a place she had no idea how to get out of, about to break into a city filled with jinni who thought very little of humans and three of them were human. No wonder her family frequently told her she was always doing something inappropriate. "How are we getting in if we're not going through the front gate?"

Luca grinned. "Over the back wall."

Penelope looked the walls up and down, comparing them to those entering the gate. "I thought you said you said you can't fly."

"Neither can you, but that'll not stop you from going over the wall." Luca tugged on her hand, drawing her forward. "Watch where I step."

The first couple of steps were easy. Penelope began to think reaching the valley would be a breeze. Her next step had loose stones skidding out from under her feet and her hand tightened on Luca's as she struggled not to fall.

He drew her upwards, waiting until she was steady before he continued. Behind them Alex and Malachi followed in single file.

By the time they reached the valley, Penelope was hot, tired, sick of sand and partially coated in it from her less than elegant descent down the mountain. A look at both Malachi and Alex showed they hadn't fared any better with the sand. It made her feel a little happier, but not by much.

Lifting her hair up off the nape of her neck, Penelope watched Luca rummage in the backpack he'd placed on the ground. "Why does it have to be so hot here?"

"We are born of fire." Luca held a one-litre bottle of water out to Penelope.

She took it, unscrewing the lid. "Doesn't all this heat bother you?" She drank nearly half the bottle before she handed it back.

"Not in the least." Luca returned the bottle to the backpack.

"Aren't you going to have a drink?" Penelope started to suggest the hunters might want a drink, but stopped when she saw them take bottles of water from their own backpacks.

"I can survive without for now." Luca swung the backpack into place. "Are you ready?"

Penelope eyed the distance they had to travel before turning and checking what they'd already crossed. She sighed. They weren't even half way. If she was honest, they weren't a quarter of the way. She faced the city. "I'm never going to be able to walk that far."

"Do you wish to have a rest first?" Luca asked.

When Penelope didn't immediately answer, Malachi spoke. "How long is it until night? Wouldn't we be better off travelling in the cool?"

"Day has the heat, lizards, snakes and centipedes. Night has scorpions, spiders and rats," Luca said.

"Neither option sounds good." Penelope glanced around, half expecting to see centipedes crawling up out of the sand nearby.

Luca stepped closer, taking Penelope's hand. "You'll not have to search to see them. If they arrive you'll know it."

"Why?" She couldn't resist asking the question even though she dreaded the answer.

"They are larger than what you're accustomed to. They remain outside the walls of the city and the jinni rarely venture outside the gates. In a way they protect the city from anyone who wishes to enter."

Penelope's heart sank. "Like us."

Luca tightened his hand on hers. "I'll protect you."

She was getting a little tired of hearing those words. She wanted to be able to protect herself. Like Cassidy could. "When all this is over, I want you to teach me to fight." She glanced at the sword hanging at his side.

"What use would learning how to use a sword be to you?"

"She could be a hunter," Malachi said.

"It takes more than skill with a sword to become a hunter," Alex said.

She faced the hunters, keeping hold of Luca's hand. "What else does it take?"

Malachi glanced skywards before he spoke. "The sun is getting lower and that conversation is too long to finish before dark." He grinned. "If we survive, ask us when we return home."

Penelope tried to push away the fear that threatened to swamp her. "You don't think we'll survive?"

Malachi shrugged, a smile still in place. "We're not immortal." He glanced towards Luca. "Unlike some."

"After this journey I'll not be immortal either." Luca glanced towards the city. "Do we rest or travel on?"

"Travel on. At least in the day we can see what's coming for us," Alex said.

His words made Penelope dread the coming night. "What will we do when the sun sets?" She walked beside Luca who headed towards the city, the hunters on the other side of her.

"Be vigilant."

She glared at Luca. His answer hadn't been helpful.

"What is wrong?" Luca glanced at her.

"Nothing." She looked away from him when he smiled.

They fell silent as they walked towards the city, the

sun creeping closer to the mountains. Several times they stopped for short breaks to have a drink and once to have something to eat. More than once Luca hurried them off in another direction, warning them it wasn't safe to continue on the path they were on. Penelope didn't ask him what they avoided, deciding it was safer not to know. The sun had nearly set behind the mountains when Luca stopped abruptly, looking in several directions.

"What can you hear?" Alex asked.

"Do you wish to face a lizard or snake?"

"Why are you hesitating?" Penelope demanded. "Which direction is the lizard?"

"If he's hesitating then it probably isn't a simple answer," Alex said.

Malachi's hands went to the hilts of his swords. "What's the difference?"

"One has fangs, the other has claws."

Penelope's mouth dropped open for a second. "Since when do lizards have claws?"

"Since they encountered the jinni." Luca checked over his shoulder. "If you don't wish to face the lizard we should move now before it comes any closer and realises we're here."

"Snake." Penelope looked in the direction Luca had checked. Surely fangs had to be better than claws.

"This way." Luca changed their direction, drawing his sword and walking ahead of her.

Chapter Eighteen

Penelope wasn't in the slightest bit tempted to walk beside Luca. Fangs might have sounded better than claws, but that didn't mean she wanted to face them. A glance towards the hunters showed they too had drawn weapons. Her hand momentarily rested on the hilt of the dagger. She left it sheathed. It was pointless drawing it when she had no idea how to use it.

Luca ran ahead, a blur of movement. Alex and Malachi shared a look, Malachi glancing at Penelope before nodding towards Alex, who gave a single nod. Malachi ran after Luca, leaving Alex behind, their exchange having taken only seconds.

Penelope walked quicker, her feet and legs protesting. A pity Luca wasn't the sort of jinn to grant wishes. "You two have fought together before."

Alex nodded.

"He talks a lot more than you."

Alex grinned fleetingly. "Most of my family do."

She looked into his solemn eyes. "Why are you sad?"

"Not being quick to smile doesn't necessarily make a person sad."

"But you are, aren't you?" She recognised the expression she saw in his eyes. Only because she'd seen it so often in her own. But at least in his eyes she'd never seen a lack of hope like she'd seen in hers, far too many times to count.

"Occasionally." He shrugged. "No one is happy all the time."

She wanted to argue it was more than that, but he obviously wasn't about to tell her. Not that she blamed him. She supposed she was as much a stranger to him as he was to her. Before she could say anything, she heard the sound of a sword striking something ahead of them. "That didn't sound like a snake." But it hadn't sounded like metal either. She broke into a run, fearing something else had joined the fight, gritting her teeth against the ache in her legs.

Even though the land appeared flat, there were hollows and rises and she hurried up the rise, pausing at the top when she saw the snake Luca and Malachi fought. Alex ran past her, his sword out, joining the battle. Penelope remained on the rise, her mouth gaping and her gaze fixed on the snake that towered over her companions.

The body of the snake had to be thicker than her own body and it was at least two, if not three times her height. Large fangs protruded from its mouth and the sound she'd heard earlier was that of a sword connecting with a fang, blocking it when the snake struck. Luca attacked the snake from all sides, a blur of movement the snake found impossible to track. Yet it managed to avoid most of the blows. Including Luca's. When Alex joined the fight, the attacks coming from three different directions at once, the snake was soon unable to avoid being struck. Twisting away, the snake burrowed in the sand, disappearing from view.

Penelope remained on the rise, staring at the sand as it fell back into place, all evidence of the snake's existence gone.

"Run!"

Before Penelope could ask Luca why, the snake burst from the ground in front of her. She didn't have time to reach for the dagger hanging at her side before Luca was pushing her out of the way and attacking the snake. She stumbled back, her gaze fixed on the snake, her heart racing.

Alex and Malachi joined Luca and this time when the snake burrowed beneath the sand it didn't return. They stayed where they were, scanning the area, swords remaining in their hands.

Penelope took a step closer to Luca. "Is it gone?"

"It has stayed in the area."

"Time for us to go then." Malachi glanced at the sky. "And if at all possible, how about we avoid snakes in future. The lizard sounds like it was probably the better option."

Luca took Penelope's hand, walking towards the city. "They are equally fierce."

"I'm beginning to think demons are the easier opponent." Malachi sheathed one of his swords.

Penelope feared she agreed. Which was a worry since it was demons that had killed her. She tightened her grip on Luca, meeting his gaze when she noticed he looked in her direction. She could almost feel him asking her what was wrong. Unable to answer, she looked away. The list of what was wrong would be long. But for once, there were also things that were right.

When the sun slid behind the mountains, darkness settling over the land, the hunters took out torches from their backpacks, turning them on. They'd sheathed their swords when Luca had sheathed his, continuing to warily look around the area.

Penelope stared off into the darkness, wishing she'd thought to check the distance they'd travelled compared to the distance they had to go before it had grown too dark to see. Above her stars glittered in the sky, none of the constellations appearing familiar. Not that she knew many other than the Southern Cross and the Big Dipper. Luca, who continued to hold her hand, squeezed it lightly. She looked towards him, but there were too many shadows to clearly see his expression. The hunters kept their torches pointed at the ground.

Eventually Luca called a halt. They stopped in a hollow that had both a waterhole and a tumble of rocks that they huddled amongst to sleep, Luca remaining on watch. Penelope barely managed not to beg the hunters to turn a torch on when they'd turned them off, lying down to sleep back to back. Not expecting to be able to sleep, Penelope closed her eyes, exhaustion causing her to fall instantly asleep.

Feeling a hand on her shoulder, she came abruptly awake, her heart racing, the scream that had nearly escaped stopped when she saw Luca leaned over her. It took her a few more seconds to realise light was starting to fill the sky.

"I didn't mean to scare you."

She reached up to run her hand along his jaw, sliding past his ear to cup the back of his head and tug him forward. His lips barely brushed across hers before he was pulling back. She made a sound in protest, sitting up.

He kept his voice low. "I'd not have them think badly of you for being with a jinn."

She slid her hands around his neck. "I don't care what they think." Her lips met his and this time he returned her kiss with more than a brush of his lips. When she eventually drew back, she smiled up at him. "Good morning."

He returned her smile. "Let us hope it remains good." He rose to his feet, holding out a hand.

Taking it, she let him help her rise. Once on her feet, she stretched, rubbing at a few of the aching places that felt worse than they had been when she'd gone to sleep. Her gaze was drawn to the city. She stared at it for a moment, wondering how they were going to get over the wall, before she turned and faced the direction they'd come from. She checked the city again, wanting to make sure. Smiling, she again looked at the distance they'd travelled. They were closer to the city than the mountains. It finally felt like they were getting somewhere.

After a quick breakfast, a drink from the waterhole and wishing there was a toilet when she found out she'd have to use the bushes on the other side of the waterhole, Penelope reluctantly agreed it was time to continue. She stared at the city ahead, glad they hadn't been disturbed by any creatures during the night. If a snake was approximately three times the size of her, she dreaded to think how big a scorpion or spider would be. Or a rat. She shuddered.

"Would you answer me if I asked what is wrong?"

"What do we have to face in the resting place of Solomon?" It better not be a rat larger than herself.

"Several creatures," Luca said.

Penelope began to worry if she should continue to ask. Maybe it'd be better not to know rather than stress about them the rest of the way to the city. "Name one of them."

"A winged lion."

She stumbled. "I think I'd prefer the rat."

Malachi chuckled. "You and me both. I'm also betting the lion won't be the size of your typical lion."

"Was that a rhetorical question or were you expecting an answer?" Luca asked.

"Great," Penelope muttered. Luca's comment had

been more than enough of an answer. "Why can't there be tiny creatures around here?"

"How would you fight a creature you could barely see?" Alex asked.

"Oh."

Luca squeezed her hand. "She would not need to fight it. I'd protect her."

She nearly growled at hearing those words. She wanted to say she could look out for herself. But it obviously wasn't true. Memories of saltwater burning down her throat returned. Nowhere near true. She looked around, desperate for a distraction. There was only sand and the city ahead of them. "How are we going to get over the wall?"

"Grappling hook and rope."

"Where are you going to get them from?"

"My backpack."

"Oh." Luckily one of them had known what to bring. She hadn't had a single clue about what they'd face. Not that she knew much more of what was to come.

Luca lightly squeezed her hand. "It will soon be over and you can return to your life."

She wanted to protest his words, but remained quiet as they headed towards the city. There were some things she wanted over, but others she didn't.

Her grip tightened on Luca's hand. What if he didn't feel the same way?

They reached the rear wall of the city late morning, having had to avoid numerous creatures and take a large detour around the city to steer clear of the main gates. While Luca rummaged in his backpack, Penelope's gaze slowly travelled up the wall to the top of it.

"You do realise I'm not very athletic, don't you?" Penelope faced Luca.

Luca straightened, a rope and grappling hook in his hands. "I'll tie the rope around your waist and draw you up once I'm on top of the wall."

It didn't sound much better, but unable to come up with any other options, she remained silent. Standing near the hunters, she watched as Luca threw the hook, tugging so it caught hold of the top of the wall.

Luca faced Alex. "Tie the rope around Penelope once I reach the top." When Alex nodded, Luca started up the rope.

She hadn't expected him to be able to move so quickly while climbing a rope. It had seemed impossible. But he was a blur of movement, pausing at the top of the wall to peer over. A few seconds later he was on top of it gesturing for them to send Penelope up.

She lifted up her arms so Alex could tie the rope around her.

Finished, Alex took one of her hands and placed it on the rope. "Hold on and try and keep yourself away from the wall by using your feet. It'll make it easier for you instead of being banged against the wall."

Nodding, she held onto where he'd indicated and looked up at Luca. She sent him a wave of emotions to let him know she was ready. They weren't exactly the ones she'd planned to send. Along with the reassurance was fear. The rope tightened and she was jerked upwards. It took her a few seconds to remember to use her feet to push herself away from the wall, doing something that probably looked like an odd walk.

She tried not to look down as the top of the wall came closer, but she couldn't resist. Her grip tightened on the rope as she reminded herself that Luca wouldn't let her fall.

His hands reached for her, helping her sit on the top of the wall so he could undo the rope. "You're unharmed?"

She nodded, clinging to the top of the wall. It was a lot wider than she'd expected it to be, but too narrow for her peace of mind.

Luca dropped the end of the rope over the side and

gestured for the next one to come up. Alex slowly climbed the rope.

Chapter Nineteen

Penelope looked away before Alex was halfway up the rope, unable to watch the slow progress. That was how fast she'd expected Luca to go up the rope. A speed that meant she'd be stuck on the top of the wall far too long. She looked at the city spread out below, trying to take her mind off her location. It wasn't the height that bothered her. It was sitting in plain view of a city full of jinni.

Her gaze roamed over the flat roofed buildings. Some were single storey boxes, while others rose several storeys high and some were built around courtyards filled with potted plants and fountains. Many of the roads between the buildings were paved, a scattering of sand across them. Other areas were expanses of sand, like the area directly below them, which was surprising since the nearby building was rather impressive with a peaked roof, columns and carvings on some of the walls. Her mouth dropped open as she stared at a jinn walking across the sand.

Penelope wanted to tell Luca, but feared the jinn would hear her. Keeping her gaze on the jinn, she reached out and tugged on Luca's arm, trying to keep her emotions neutral so he didn't ask her what was wrong. Still watching below, she pressed a finger against her lips in the hope that Luca was looking at her and understood the message. Barely moving at all, she pointed below.

Luca pressed her against the top of the wall, drawing her towards the outer edge. Keeping low himself, he looked from one side of the wall to the other.

Penelope felt his fear for a split second and wished she could ask him what was wrong. Had the jinn spotted them? She discarded that thought immediately. Looking in the other direction, she saw Alex was nearly at the top. Then she spotted it, the reason for Luca's fear.

A snake slithered towards Malachi, his back to it, the creature a good distance from him. Luca dropped a small piece of the wall, which he'd crumbled off the edge, onto Malachi. When the hunter looked at him, Luca pressed a finger to his lips then pointed in the direction of the snake. Luca threw another small piece of the wall at Malachi when he started to draw his weapons.

Penelope could see Malachi's confusion when Luca shook his head. She checked in the other direction, ducking back when she noticed the jinn remained in the area. Her heart raced as she checked Malachi, seeing the snake was now several metres away.

Alex reached the top of the wall, pulling himself up and laying across it like they were. He stared down at his cousin, gesturing for him to come up.

Penelope had no idea how he could remain calm. It took all her self-control to stay quiet and not yell at Malachi to hurry up. She drew in a sharp breath when the snake struck out at Malachi, who was climbing the rope.

Malachi pushed away from the wall, causing the rope to swing sideways, the snake barely missing him. He managed another metre before the snake struck again. This time he swung out in the other direction, spinning so his back hit the wall. He kicked out at the snake that came for him once more. The snake reared back and Malachi scrambled further up the rope. He wasn't out of reach when the snake struck. He slid down the rope, the snake's fangs striking the wall above him.

Penelope winced, looking over the other side of

the wall to see if the jinn had heard the noise. Her breath rushed out when she couldn't see him. "He's gone." She looked back at Malachi.

The snake reared. Luca rose to his feet, grabbing hold of the rope and hauling it up. He managed to get Malachi past the snake, the fangs once again biting into the wall. The next time the snake struck, Malachi was well out of reach.

Shaking, Penelope rested her head against the top of the wall, closing her eyes. She quickly opened them when she saw the snake strike over and over again in her mind. Snakes had never bothered her before or, more accurately, she'd never cared either way. She had a feeling they'd probably feature rather prominently in future nightmares. Along with drowning.

Malachi reached the top of the wall. "You couldn't have pulled me up earlier?"

Luca tossed the rope over the other side. "There was someone below. I couldn't risk them catching sight of us."

Penelope noticed the rope was tied to a ring pushed into the top of the wall, the grappling hook nowhere in sight. She supposed it was in Luca's backpack. "How are we meant to get down the other side?"

Luca grinned. "Were you not the one who

reminded me I cannot fly?" He turned to Alex and Malachi. "Who will go first?"

Malachi took hold of the rope. "I'm not about to go last again." He slipped over the edge, making his way down the rope.

Penelope gestured towards Malachi. "I can't do that."

"I can lower you down as easily as I pulled you up," Luca said.

"And after that? Where is Solomon's resting place?"

Luca nodded towards the building below them. "In the temple. Where else would you lay the dead to rest?"

She stared at the building. "We're about to raid a church?"

Luca chuckled softly. "We'll only take that which belongs to me. There'll be no raiding involved."

"What about the winged lion you mentioned? Where is it?"

"They're in the temple. There'll be no raiding, but there will be fighting. Only the determined can reach the inner chamber."

His words were not in the least reassuring. Before she could tell him, Malachi reached the ground and Luca drew up the rope to tie it around her waist. She grabbed hold of his hands before he could lower her. "How will we get out of this place when you're human?"

"The same way we got into it." He lowered her over the edge.

She clutched the rope, pushing away from the wall with her feet. The ground slowly came closer and Malachi reached for her, steadying her as she tried to stand up. She was surprised to find she was still shaky from watching the snake attack Malachi. Her fingers fumbled on the rope, trying to undo the knot.

"Let me." Malachi brushed her hands away.

"Weren't you scared?"

"When?"

"When the snake was attacking you."

"I was too focused on surviving to be scared." He finished undoing the knot and let the rope fall back against the wall.

"And now? Are you scared now?"

Malachi grinned. "Now I can't wait to find out what's in the temple. I'll worry about being scared later."

"Are you saying that, or do you mean it?"

Alex dropped onto the ground beside them, letting go of the rope. "He means it. His lack of fear is the reason he has no hunting partner and is stuck on clean up duty."

Malachi's grin didn't falter. "Of course it's not the reason. It's fear that keeps other hunters from being my partner."

Penelope looked at each of the hunters. "What do they fear?"

"Running headlong into danger," Alex said.

"You're wrong. I never go running into danger." Malachi's grin widened. "I go swinging my swords and returning demons to hell."

Luca joined them on the ground. "There are no demons to return to hell around here. But there will be danger and battles to be won."

Malachi drew his swords. "That's why I'm here."

Luca looked at each of them. "There's only one entrance into the temple and it's through the front. There'll be four winged lions. Be careful of their teeth and claws. There are two cockatrices whose gazes have the ability to paralyse. It can be used against them if you hold a mirror in front of their face. There are two polished bronze mirrors in the main chamber that can be used for that purpose. And lastly, there's a manticore. Beware of its scorpion tail. Not only does it sting like a scorpion, but it also shoots venomous spines."

Penelope reached for the nearby wall, resting her hand against the dusty sandstone. "What's in the next chamber?" How were they meant to get past all those creatures? Was Luca crazy?

"Don't touch the tomb and you'll have nothing to fear in the next chamber."

"Tomb?"

"It looks like a stone coffin."

"Oh." She twisted a strand of hair between her fingers. She wasn't ready for this. She probably never would be.

"Where will we find the other half of your medallion?" Alex asked.

"In the second chamber. There will be a pile of them." Luca removed his watch and took the back off it, separating the half a medallion from the setting. He held it out to Penelope. "Call for me before you fit them back together. I need to be there too."

She nodded, taking the medallion and pushing it deep inside a pocket of her jeans. There was no way she wanted to lose it.

Luca faced the hunters. "One of you will fight with me while the other will help Penelope."

Malachi grinned. "Alex can help Penelope."

His words didn't surprise her. "What about when you join me in the second chamber? You can't expect Malachi to fight on his own."

"It'll not take long to fit the halves of the medallion

back together. By then we should have reduced the amount of creatures that'll be attacking us." Luca took her hand, the one that had been pressed against the wall. "Are you ready?" He dusted the sand from her palm.

She almost said no. A manticore that could shoot venomous spines didn't sound like something she wanted to meet. She met his gaze, seeing the hope in his eyes. The word remained unspoken and she nodded.

Luca drew her closer. "Thank you." His words were soft. "I'd begun to fear this day would never arrive." He held her gaze a moment longer before he lightly pressed his lips against hers, stepping back and drawing her with him. "Wait until we have the creatures distracted before you make a run for the far room. Keep to the edges and try and remain out of sight."

She nodded, clinging to his hand. She wasn't crazy enough to run headlong into danger. Her gaze was momentarily drawn to Malachi, who followed them, Alex walking beside him. She was half tempted to ask Alex why he'd invited Malachi along, but feared it was because there'd been no one crazy enough to join them.

Luca stopped at the corner of the building, letting

go of Penelope's hand so he could dash ahead and check the way was clear. He gestured them forward, leading the way up a set of wide stairs.

They entered the building between two columns that towered over them, stepping into the cool interior that was lit by numerous hanging oil lamps. For a few seconds the immense size of the place took all of Penelope's attention. The ceiling had to be at least fifteen metres above her, the room nearly thirty metres wide and over fifty metres long. The floor was quarried stone and the walls covered in carved frescoes, each depicting different scenes. There were large statues lined up along each side of the room, some of them nearly tall enough to touch the ceiling. Her awe was replaced by fear when two winged lions strode towards them.

Alex drew Penelope to the side of the chamber tugging her behind a large statue. "I think we can make it to the next statue without catching their attention."

Penelope pressed herself against the statue, not wanting to move away from the safety of it. "They had faces. Human faces."

"I know."

"With sharp teeth." She closed her eyes, trying to force the horrifying image from her mind. She'd expected a lion that would look like a lion, not some human-animal hybrid with wings that could have belonged to a bat. An extremely large bat.

Alex placed a hand on her shoulder. "We need to get to the other chamber."

She opened her eyes to stare at him. "Luca said there are four. Where are the rest of them? And the other creatures?"

"They'll hear the noise and join the fight. If we remain quiet we should be able to sneak past everything."

"They'll be outnumbered." She couldn't bring herself to move.

Alex nodded. "All the more reason to start moving."

She wanted to tell him to stop sounding so rational. There was nothing rational about this situation. "What if we run into one of them? I can't fight."

Alex smiled fleetingly. "I can. If we run into one, you make your way to the second chamber and I'll join you as soon as possible."

"That doesn't sound like a good plan."

"Neither does remaining behind this statue when all that noise could draw the attention of something from outside the temple." He gestured in the direction of the fight.

She pushed herself away from the statue. "We're already outnumbered. We wouldn't cope with any more."

"Do you want me to go first?"

She shook her head. Not wanting to be left behind. "Together." She eyed the distance between them and the next statue.

"Okay. On the count of three."

Chapter Twenty

It took Penelope a few seconds to reply. "Okay." She tried not to focus on the sounds of battle. They made her want to run in the opposite direction.

"One. Two. Three."

She ran with Alex to the next statue, pressing herself against the carved white stone when she reached it. She momentarily wondered if it was made of marble, then decided it didn't matter. It kept them hidden from the creatures Luca and Malachi fought.

"Ready to run to the next one?"

Pushing away from the statue, she nodded, taking a deep breath as Alex counted once more. They continued along the edge of the room, moving from statue to statue, once hiding behind a large circle of polished bronze that Penelope guessed was the mirror Luca had mentioned. It hung from a carved timber frame, looking more like a gong than a mirror.

Reaching the far statue, Penelope peered around it. There were no hiding places between them and the doorway.

"It's about ten metres to the doorway of the second chamber." Alex peered around the other side of the statue. "It looks like all the creatures are near the temple entrance."

Penelope looked past him. "How can you tell?" None of them remained still. Not Luca and Malachi and not the creatures.

"I can't for certain. Are you ready for the last sprint?"

"Not really." She pushed away from the statue. "But I guess we can't stay here." She brushed her fingers across her jeans, feeling the half a medallion in her pocket. "On the count of three?"

Alex nodded. "One. Two. Three."

Penelope ran towards the doorway, following Alex. She couldn't resist a look in Luca's direction. She stumbled when she saw a large bird like creature coming towards her, a barbed snake tail and taloned wings looking more dangerous than the sharp beak. There was no way she could get out of its way in time.

Alex stepped in front of her, his sword at the ready. "Don't look into its eyes."

She thought of the mirror. It was too large to bring to the creature.

"Fall back."

"What about you?"

The cockatrice attacked. Leaping in the air to strike at Alex with clawed feet, sharp spurs low on the rear of its legs. The barbed tail came around as it landed. Alex blocked and attacked, slowly driven backwards, unable to answer as he fought the constant attacks of the creature.

They were forced away from the doorway and Penelope looked around for a way to help. She kept thinking of the mirror. How long could Alex keep avoiding the creature's gaze? If it paralysed him, he was dead. There was no way she could fight it. Even if she knew how to use the dagger. Something that small was no match for a creature that size. A glance behind showed the rear corner was getting closer. If they didn't change direction the cockatrice would have them pinned in the corner and dead within minutes. "This way." She headed back the way they'd come.

"Run to the second chamber."

She ignored Alex. There was no way she was about to run past the cockatrice. Malachi was the one who liked to run headlong into danger. Not her. "This way." She kept moving towards the bronze mirror, her heart racing and her gaze firmly on the floor. She nearly missed the attack when it came. Leaping back when Alex yelled at her to run, having felt the rush of air, she staggered, trying to regain her balance.

Alex again got between her and the creature, striking out at it.

The cockatrice leapt over him, going for Penelope once more. She fell as she tried to escape, rolling out of the way. The barbed tail struck the floor, chips of stone flying towards her.

Again Alex put himself between Penelope and the cockatrice.

The creature screeched loudly, the sound ringing out around them.

Penelope pressed her hands against her ears as she gained her feet, backing away. A glance behind showed the mirror was only a couple of metres away. She looked between the feet of the bird and her destination. Then she couldn't see the feet, guessing it had once again leapt in the air for an attack. Spinning, she ran towards the mirror, feeling a rush of air behind her and the sound of the cockatrice landing on the floor, its tail striking the stone.

"Move faster."

She wanted to look behind her at Alex's warning,

but feared it would slow her down. There was a gap between the bronze mirror and the floor. More than high enough for her to slide under. Feeling the rush of air, she threw herself forward, colliding with the floor and rolling the last metre. There was a crashing sound as the creature struck the bronze mirror. Penelope jumped to her feet and slammed her hand against the back of the mirror.

The screeching cry of the cockatrice was cut off in mid cry, a crashing sound coming from the other side of the mirror.

Penelope stared at the back of the mirror, breathing heavily as she waited for the next attack. It didn't come.

Alex stepped around the edge of the timber frame, a grin fleetingly appearing. "Count of three?"

She laughed, having no idea why she did. Eventually her laughter ended and she managed to speak. "What happened?"

"It looked in the mirror."

"How long will it be paralysed?"

Alex shrugged. "It's not the only creature in here."

He hadn't needed to tell her that. She could hear the fighting near the entrance of the temple. "Forget about counting." They'd been in the temple too long. She didn't want to die again. She ran along the side of the temple, headed for the far wall. When she reached it, she paused, checking the way was clear before she ran the last ten metres. This time she entered the second chamber without a problem. She came to a halt not far inside the room. A bigger problem was in front of her.

Alex stopped beside her. "I don't suppose you have some trick to make this easier."

Penelope slowly shook her head, her gaze riveted on the piles of medallions. All of them were broken in half and made of various different metals. She drew out Luca's medallion to stare at it for a moment. How was she going to find the other half? There had to be thousands of them.

"Talk about a needle in a haystack." Alex sheathed his sword and strode forward, picking up the nearest medallion half. He dropped it, drawing back as if stung.

"What happened?" She joined him.

"It felt like it burned me." He looked at the half she held. "Hold that out for a second."

"Why?" She held her hand closer to him, the medallion on her open palm.

Alex touched a finger to the medallion, instantly drawing back. "I can't touch it. I'm not sure how I'm meant to put the two halves together if I can't touch it."

Penelope frowned. "I don't-" She broke off, remembering how Luca had needed permission. "I give you permission to be able to touch the medallion. Both halves of it."

Alex reached for the medallion again, his fingers remaining above it for a few seconds before he pressed them against the metal. He took it from her palm, turning it over in his hand before giving it back. "That should make it a little easier. If it doesn't feel like we're touching the flames of a fire then we have the correct one."

She slid the medallion into her pocket, eyeing the piles in front of her. "Easier?" He obviously didn't know the meaning of the word.

Alex didn't answer. Crouching in front of a pile of medallions he lightly touched one before pushing it away from the pile.

Penelope watched him for nearly a minute before she could bring herself to do the same. Did he really think they could find a single medallion amongst all the ones in this room? It'd take them days. And she didn't think they had days. Mimicking Alex's movements, she pushed medallions away from the pile, hissing when her fingers felt like they were pressed against fire. She lost count of the amount of medallions she pushed aside, stopping after long minutes of sorting and feeling like she hadn't made the slightest dint in the pile. "This is impossible."

"Are you giving up?"

"No. But there has to be a better way than this."

"What did Luca tell you?"

"That I had to find the other half of the medallion and it'd be in this room."

"Then you better keep looking." Alex brushed another medallion from the pile.

She rose to her feet, surveying the room. It was impossible. She slipped her hand into the pocket of her jeans and pulled out the half a medallion. Utterly impossible. She strode past the piles that were gathered around the tomb in the middle of the room. "There has to be another way." She rubbed her thumb over the medallion, feeling the pattern.

"Keep looking. They're out there fighting for their lives. For our lives."

Startled by the stern tone of Alex's voice, she spun to face him, the medallion slipping from her fingers. She tried to grab it before it hit the floor and was lost amongst the other medallions. She missed. It rolled down the side of the pile it landed on, curving towards the rear of the chamber. Again she tried to grab it.

Alex grabbed hold of her hand, preventing her. "No. Look at it. That isn't natural."

Her mouth dropped open. "It shouldn't be able to roll. It isn't round." She followed it as it crossed the room, coming to a halt partway up one of the piles.

"I think you found your easier method."

She bent to pick up the half a medallion, her gaze drawn to the one it had landed next to, not quite touching it. She picked it up too. Holding both halves in front of her, centimetres separating them, she stared at the image that covered the two halves. A comet and a tower. "We need Luca."

"I'll get him."

He was nearly at the door when she remembered there was another way. "Wait." She sent her emotions to Luca. They were a muddle as she realised she had no idea what one would work best for calling him to her. It took her a few seconds to figure it out. Need. She let him know how much she needed him.

Luca entered the room in a blur of movement, stopping in front of her. "I knew you could find it."

"What do we do now?" Alex looked towards the doorway several times.

Luca gestured towards the medallion halves. "Give him permission to hold them."

"I already have."

Luca faced Alex. "Take them and while facing the tomb press them back together. Return them to Penelope and then your part is done."

Alex took the two halves of the medallion. "Then I can help Malachi?"

Luca inclined his head. "Yes."

Alex faced the tomb, pressing the two halves together, Penelope standing beside him. There was a glimmer of light across the seam. He held the medallion out to her.

She took it from him, staring at the unbroken surface as Alex ran from the chamber, his sword drawn. She ran her thumb over the image of the comet and tower. Turning it over, she did the same to the words etched on the other side. "What do they say?"

"It is my family's motto. Family. Loyalty. Courage. The inscription is in Latin. The image on the other side is our family crest. Our coat of arms."

She met his gaze. "When I saw all the medallions I thought I'd never find the right one."

"When a created jinn doesn't survive their half of

the medallion is brought here. Never to be connected to its missing half which also remains here."

She stared at the medallion she held, relieved that hadn't happened to Luca. "What do I do now?"

"Return it to me and release me from my curse."

"What do I say?"

"That I am no longer bound to you. The curse is broken, the debt paid."

Chapter Twenty-One

Penelope held the medallion out to Luca. The words stuck in her throat that ached for some reason she couldn't work out. "You are no longer bound to me." Her voice was soft, the words harder to say than she'd expected. Soon he'd leave and she feared he wouldn't return. "The curse is broken and your debt is paid." She pressed the medallion into his hand.

His fingers curled around the medallion and he smiled. "Thank you."

"That's it? You're human again?" She rested her hand against his chest, the beat of his heart strong beneath her palm. But it always had been. "How can you be sure?" She'd expected something more spectacular. Especially after having faced a cockatrice.

"I feel human." He placed a hand over hers. "I need to help Alex and Malachi. There's still a manticore and one of the winged lions out there."

She grabbed his hand when he drew it away from her. "Be careful. You're not immortal anymore."

Luca drew her to him, kissing her swiftly. "Don't go rushing into danger like Malachi does. What you did with the cockatrice was too dangerous." He kissed her again before letting her go and striding from the chamber.

She stared after him, her fingers pressed against her lips that slowly curved into a smile. For some reason she hadn't expected that. Had thought he'd draw away from her before he returned home. Her smile faded. The kisses didn't mean he'd stay. She doubted anything, or anyone, would keep him from returning home. Not with the longing she'd heard in his voice when talking about it.

Crossing the chamber she peered into the main room, seeing the three of them at the far end, fighting against the manticore. Would it follow if they left the temple? She had no idea, but the sooner they left, the better. She'd wait behind the statues by the exit so they could go the moment they'd dealt with the last creature.

Even though the rest of the creatures had been taken care of, she ran towards the far wall, feeling too exposed as she crossed the ten metres between her and the nearest statue. She pressed herself against the statue the moment she reached it, her breath coming fast. Taking a slow, deep breath didn't help. Nor did reminding herself the manticore was busy at the other end of the temple.

Mentally counting to three, she dashed to the next statue. One by one she came closer to where the cockatrice lay in front of the bronze mirror. Reaching the mirror, she stared at the back of it, trying to convince herself to keep moving. She couldn't. Not without making sure it remained paralysed. It took her nearly a minute to be able to bring herself to peer around the edge of the timber frame. She held her breath as she stared at the creature. It was motionless. Letting her breath out in a rush of air, she sprinted to the next statue. When she reached the final statue, she peered around it to see Luca on the back of the manticore.

Pressing a hand against her mouth, her other hand against her heart, she barely managed not to scream as the scorpion tail came for him. Luca leapt off the back of the manticore at the last second, rolling across the floor and coming to his feet as the creature's tail pierced its own back.

The manticore roared, the sound echoing around them and out the exit. The creature collapsed, opening its mouth for a roar that didn't come, rows of shark-like teeth catching the sunlight that reached through the door and spilled across the floor.

"We need to get out of here. That sound probably caught the attention of every jinn in the area," Alex said.

"I need to get Penelope." Luca faced the rear of the temple.

She stepped out from behind the statue, moving towards the light coming in from the doorway. "I'm here."

Luca faced her, fear filling his expression. "Run."

She hadn't taken a single step when an arm went around her waist, dragging her back against a solid body, a dagger pressing against her throat. She met Luca's gaze, wanting to apologise when she saw his expression. Why hadn't she taken her own advice to be careful?

Luca raised his sword. "Let her go. Would you hide behind someone without training instead of facing me?"

"I warned you against bringing humans into our home. And now you are one yourself."

She recognised the contempt in the voice. It was the guard who hadn't wanted to let them enter the home of the jinni.

"Do you fear facing me because all would then

know you were beaten by a human?" Luca took a step forward.

"I fear no one. Once I kill this one I will defeat the rest of you for daring to come into so sacred a place, defiling it with your presence."

Penelope thought of the dagger that hung at her side. She didn't know how to use it, but doubted that mattered. "Please let me go." She made a halfhearted effort at trying to escape, using the movement to draw the dagger from the sheath.

The jinn laughed. "Humans are weak and pathetic."

Luca raised a hand. "Don't." He stared directly at Penelope.

"You think to order me about?" The jinn's arm tightened around Penelope.

Her breath was pressed out of her lungs. It was now or never. Turning the dagger in her hand, she stabbed it into the jinn.

He roared, his grip on her loosening so she was able to drop to the floor and scurry away. When he tried to go after her, Luca was in front of him, swinging his sword.

Alex helped Penelope to her feet, drawing her further away from the fight. "Are you okay?"

She nodded. "Help Luca."

Alex smiled. It lasted a little longer than his usual smile. "I don't think he'd appreciate it."

Before she could ask why, she was pulled away from Alex, Luca's arms going around her, holding her nearly as tightly as the jinn had held her. This time she didn't mind. Dropping the dagger, she held onto him equally as tight, her lips meeting his.

"We better leave," Alex said.

"It might be safer in here."

Penelope drew away from Luca to see Malachi peered out the doorway. "Why?"

"Jinni are headed this way."

"We can't take on an entire city." Luca scooped up the dagger and handed it to Penelope. "We stand a better chance in the desert." He strode for the door, looking outside when he reached it. "We need to make a run for it." After sheathing his sword, he dropped his backpack on the floor and rummaged around in it.

Penelope stopped partway to the door when she saw what he took out. "Are those grenades?"

Luca swung the backpack into place, keeping hold of two grenades. "Yes. Run to the left and head behind the building. Two of you go over the wall, one remain on top to lower the rope for me. I'll keep the jinni busy."

She couldn't take her gaze from the grenades. "Where did you get them from?" There was no way she could have ever expected to see one other than in a movie.

"Penelope."

She met Luca's gaze. "What?"

"Run."

Alex grabbed hold of her hand, tugging her outside with him, Malachi on their heels. They were partway along the side of the temple when there was an explosion. They didn't hear a second explosion until they reached the wall. Alex headed up first, Malachi remaining with Penelope, his swords in his hands.

Penelope stared at the back of the temple, clouds of dust hanging in the air beyond it. "Do you think Luca is okay?"

The rope jerked around, catching their attention, and they looked up to see Alex was on top of the wall. He waved Penelope up.

Malachi sheathed his swords before he tied the rope around her waist. "Put your dagger away."

She slid it into the sheath, trying not to look at the dark stains on the blade. "Do you think Luca's okay?"

Malachi stepped back, meeting her gaze. "I'd say he's had a lot of experience at this kind of thing." He looked up at Alex and gave him a thumbs up.

Penelope grabbed hold of the rope as Alex pulled her upwards. The trip wasn't as smooth as it had been when Luca had been the one pulling her up. Crashing against the wall she used her feet to help keep herself away from it. Another explosion sounded and she grinned in relief, nearly laughing at the thought that such a noise sounded good to her. It hopefully meant Luca was alive.

Alex helped her up on top of the wall, untying the rope and dropping it over the side for Malachi. He lay flat, gesturing for Penelope to do the same.

She did after she'd had a look in the direction of the temple, unable to see Luca. There was a group of jinni clustered behind a building not far from the temple, a pile of rubble between the two buildings. "How will he know it's time to head to the wall?"

"I'm sure he'll figure it out," Alex said.

Malachi spoke from below them. "I'd be more worried about what happens when he runs out of grenades. We better hope he has more than the ones he's already thrown."

She looked over the edge of the wall to see him coming closer, slowly climbing up the rope. "I doubt Luca will have enough to keep them from following us once we're over the wall." She looked upwards, surprised to see how low the sun was. "Can all jinni see in the dark?"

Malachi reached the top of the wall. "You're asking the wrong people. We're demon hunters. We don't know much about the jinni." He tossed the rope over the other side, checking out the area before lowering himself over the edge.

When another explosion sounded behind her, Penelope turned to look at the city. A larger cloud of dust hung in the air, making it impossible to see much. She checked all around the temple, looking for Luca. She couldn't see him.

A few minutes later, Alex drew up the rope and turned to her. "Your turn."

She held up her arms so he could tie it around her waist. "I really wish I'd been more interested in sports. I'm getting sick of being hauled up and down this wall." Movement caught her attention. She saw Luca run towards the wall. "Get the rope off me. Luca needs it."

Alex shook his head. "It'll be a fast trip down the side."

She half fell over the edge, grabbing at the rope as Alex lowered her. Several times she banged into the wall, spinning at the end of the rope and unable to keep herself from hitting the wall.

Malachi undid the rope when she reached the ground. "What's the hurry?"

"Luca is waiting for the rope." She watched as Alex drew it up, her hands clasped together as she waited to see Luca appear above them. It seemed to take longer than she expected before she saw him. Her legs threatened to give way and she took a few halting steps to the wall, leaning against it. When the rope snaked down the wall beside her, she moved further along, not wanting to be in the way.

Alex came down first, Luca following once Alex had reached the ground. They left the rope behind as they headed towards the mountains. Penelope clung to Luca's hand, struggling to keep up with his pace.

She glanced behind them. "How many grenades have you got left?"

"One."

"Oh."

He squeezed her hand. "You don't need to worry. I have a plan."

"Which is?"

"We'll go towards where I heard a large cluster of lizards this morning. If we are lucky it'll be a nest of them."

Chapter Twenty-Two

Penelope stumbled, tightening her grip on Luca's hand. "That doesn't sound like a plan." Nor did she think finding overgrown lizards would make them lucky. If anything, it was likely to be the complete opposite of lucky. Probably something far worse than unlucky.

"He never said it was a good plan," Malachi said.

"The jinni will hear them and believe we do not know they're in the area."

"Which means what?"

"They'll stay back, expecting the lizards to take care of us."

That was what she'd feared. "Won't they?"

"Only if we disturb them."

"We might want to pick up the pace." Malachi broke into a run.

The rest of them followed his lead, Penelope

glancing behind, regretting it immediately. They had angled away from the city and she was able to see jinni pouring out the front gate.

Penelope didn't know if there was any point in running. The twenty or so jinni would soon catch them. "Why aren't they going faster?"

"So they can watch us run," Luca said.

"That doesn't make sense." She couldn't think of anything less entertaining than watching someone run.

"Tormenting their prey," Malachi said. "Like a demon would do."

"Oh."

"How far away are the lizards?" Alex asked.

"We'll have to slow down in a few minutes," Luca said.

"They'll know something is wrong if we do that," Alex said.

"Not if Penelope behaves like she has a stitch in her side," Luca said.

She glared at him. "Why me? Why not one of you three?"

"You look the least fit of the three of us," Luca said.

"What if the jinni heard our plans? If they can hear the lizards ahead of us, why haven't they heard what we're talking about?" Penelope demanded.

"Sound travels better through the ground than the air. They'd have felt the vibrations."

She liked Luca's plan less by the minute. "What happens after my fake stitch?"

"We be quiet and tread softly. It's late enough in the day the lizards should be sleeping, soaking in the last of the heat to keep themselves warm through the night."

"What if the lizards hear us? What if they wake up?" She began to think he wasn't going to answer.

"Running is a waste of time. They can outrun you."

She opened her mouth to demand what she should do. But he'd already answered her. She closed her mouth. There was nothing she could do. Running was a waste of time and she didn't know how to fight. For a second she relived the moment when she'd stabbed the jinn. That hadn't been fighting. It had been desperation. So had been paralysing the cockatrice.

"It's time."

She glanced at him blankly before realising what he meant. Clutching at her side, she came to a staggering halt, complaining she couldn't go on even though the jinni probably couldn't hear her. Luca and the hunters clustered around her, Luca putting an arm around her waist and urging her forward at a slower pace.

Alex and Malachi drew their swords, walking softly beside them as they glanced around. Malachi kept looking behind, walking backwards as he faced the jinni.

Penelope checked to see what the jinni were doing. They'd stopped following. Some stood with their arms crossed over their chests, others with their stance wide and hands on their hips. A couple paced, curved swords drawn, mirthless grins on their faces. She looked away, trying not to think about what it meant when they didn't follow.

Luca drew her back, holding up a hand to halt the hunters. He pointed at a rock barely visible in the sand, a smooth curved surface. He mouthed the word 'lizard'.

Penelope stared at him, shaking her head in disbelief.

Luca made a motion with his hand, reminiscent of a snake slithering past.

Her legs wanted to give way when the hunters nodded and made their way around the lizard, cutting across in front of it to avoid another one. She wanted to ask what the creatures were doing, but knew speaking was a really bad idea. She'd expected the lizards to be lying on top of the sand, not half buried in it. The hunters changed direction and as she drew closer, she saw it was another lizard. She momentarily closed her eyes, her heart racing and her breathing shallow as she forced herself to step softly. All she wanted to do was run. Her legs ached with the need. She looked towards the sun, seeing it was steadily growing closer to the mountains. They had to be past the lizards before dark. What if the torches disturbed the creatures?

They made their way steadily through the partly submerged lizards, the hunters taking the lead, pointing out each one they saw. Penelope lost count after thirty. She also lost track of time, having no idea how much had passed, knowing only that the shadows were growing longer. Luca was crazy taking them this way. She glanced at him, surprised he could smile at her reassuringly as they passed yet another partly buried lizard. A glance over her shoulder showed nothing. She looked around the area, unable to see the jinni.

Luca touched her on the shoulder, waiting until she looked at him before he mimicked walking down a slope.

She nodded, letting him know she understood the jinni might be there, waiting to see what had happened. Or they might have grown bored and left, expecting the lizards to have taken care of them. They had no way of knowing until they reached the next rise.

There was the sound of shifting sands and Luca grabbed hold of Penelope's arm, drawing her close, keeping her from moving. He held up his hand when the hunters looked towards him. None of them moved, remaining still as the sound of shifting sand continued.

She barely dared turning her head, doing so a fraction at a time. She nearly missed it. The lizard burrowed deeper under the sand, hiding itself from view. Drawing in a shaky breath, she held onto Luca. What if they stepped on one of them? There was no way to tell where they were. When the sounds finally stopped, Luca tried to step away from Penelope. She clung to him, shaking her head and mouthing the word 'no'.

He smiled momentarily, pointing to a slight hollow in the sand. Taking her hand, he drew her around it, pointing out another one to her and the hunters. Their steps were slower as they continued towards the mountains, Luca shaking his head when Alex reached for his backpack.

Alex mimed using a torch.

Luca shook his head again.

Penelope eyed the sun that was half behind the mountains. If Luca didn't let them get the torches out soon, they wouldn't be able to see where they were going.

Luca waited until the last of the sun sank behind the mountains before he carefully took a torch from first Alex's backpack and then from Malachi's. After they'd travelled about another hour, he finally spoke, keeping his voice low. "We should be past them. We can stop for a few minutes and have something to eat. Tonight we'll not be able to rest. When the sun rises the jinni will check to see what happened to us."

Penelope started to say she wasn't hungry. Her stomach growled. She guessed her body had other ideas. Taking the water bottle Luca held out to her, she had a long drink. She'd wanted to ask for one ages ago, but had been terrified the lizards would have heard. It had been bad enough when Luca had taken out the torches. Every slight sound he'd made getting them out of the backpacks had made her heart leap and fear race through her.

After they'd eaten, they continued to trudge through the night, their steps growing slower. They reached the foot of the mountains a little before daybreak and Luca allowed them to rest rather than risk climbing up to the tunnel in the dark.

She leaned against Luca where they sat with their backs to the sandstone, staring at his face. "You're tired."

"It feels good. An old friend I've not known for far too many centuries." He slid his arm around her shoulders.

Malachi was stretched out on the sand, his hands behind his head, one of his swords drawn and resting at his side. "Thanks for inviting me along. It's been interesting. And fun."

"There's more fun to come."

Penelope pulled away from Luca. "What do you mean?" Surely they were nearly out of this place.

"A jinn will guard the exit."

Her heart sank. She hadn't expected there to be another one, but guessed it made sense. "How are we meant to get past him?"

"Or her," Luca corrected.

"Well?" she demanded.

"We'll keep the guard busy while you open the tunnel. You need to place your hand against the stone wall and say, 'I entered of my own free will, granted passage into the home of the jinni. I leave of my own free will, returning to the mortal world I left behind.'

Don't take your hand off the stone or the tunnel will stop opening. Once you let go, we'll have five minutes for all of us to run through the tunnel before it closes. Unlike the jinni you don't have the power to hold the entrance open for as long as necessary."

"Will that be enough time?" Alex asked.

Penelope had been about to ask the exact same question.

"If we're quick."

That was what she'd feared. There was no time for anything to go wrong. She sighed heavily. "Something is sure to go wrong. It always does."

Luca drew her back against him. "Rest while you can."

She would rather he told her that everything would work out. Not make her worry more. She drifted off to sleep, groaning when Luca woke her, light beginning to fill the sky.

Malachi echoed her groan. "I could do with a cup of coffee." He stretched. "Make that two cups."

Alex rummaged in his backpack, taking out a bottle of water. "I could do with a decent sleep."

Luca handed Penelope a bottle of water and a breakfast bar. "We need to continue in a couple of minutes."

The thought of what was ahead of them made

the food taste like dust. Or maybe sand. Between the sand, that felt like it coated her skin and had burrowed into her clothes, and being drowned in the ocean she doubted she'd want to go anywhere near a beach in the near future. Finished the breakfast bar, she drank half the bottle of water before handing it back to Luca. She watched as he finished off the bottle, having already eaten a breakfast bar. A smile formed at the reminders of his humanity.

Luca took hold of her hand. "You're happy?"

She grinned at his confusion. "You're human. We managed to break the curse." There'd been more than a couple of times when she'd doubted they would.

He returned her grin. "Yes. We broke the curse."

She continued to stare at him a moment longer, not moving until Alex reminded them the jinni would be coming after them. She reluctantly let go of Luca's hand.

Chapter Twenty-Three

It took a couple of hours to reach the opening of the tunnel where they paused for a drink of water. They stood in the entrance, sand swirling across the ground from the hot breeze that entered the tunnel, doing nothing to reduce the heat of the morning. Below they saw a handful of jinni returning to the city from the direction of the lizards.

Once the jinni had entered the city, they turned and trudged along the tunnel, Penelope walking beside Luca holding his hand, the hunters behind them with their torches. "I forgot how long this tunnel was." Remembering Malachi's comment in the vehicle, she said, "If this is what camping is all about no wonder we never went."

Luca chuckled softly. "Camping is different to this. I'll take you one day so you can know the difference."

She tried to think of something to say other than

demands for him to stay in her life for more than a single camping trip. Her gaze was drawn to the walls of the tunnel, noticing they'd changed from the lighter coloured sandstone to the greyish stone that meant they were nearing the end.

Luca let go of her hand to take a battery-powered lantern from his backpack. He held it out to Penelope, leaving it turned off.

"Why didn't we use this earlier?" She took the lantern from him, wondering if she should turn it on.

"We'll not be able to hold a torch while fighting. Place the lantern somewhere that'll give all of us light. Wait until the last moment to turn it on as it's bright and drains the batteries quicker than a torch."

At the reminder of the upcoming fight, she remained silent.

"What is wrong?"

She couldn't resist smiling at Luca's words. "Going to the home of the jinni might have been dangerous, but it helped me figure something else out. Not only do I hate waiting, but I also don't like to stand back and let other people protect me."

"That's something we can fix. You can easily learn to fight."

"How do you know I can easily learn?" Every single muscle in her body ached and it was an effort to place one foot in front of the other. That didn't sound like someone who'd be able to fight.

"I've trained numerous warriors over the centuries. You have something many of them didn't have."

She doubted it very much. "What's that?"

"Perseverance when it counts. You kept going, even in the face of great danger."

There'd been far too many times in her life when she'd given up. Had he forgotten? She didn't bother reminding him of her failings. Not while the hunters listened.

"Humans," a voice said from ahead, disgust in his tone.

Penelope turned on the lantern, the light from it reaching a lot further than that of the torches. She stared at the guard who strode towards them. He looked different to the previous one. Although he wasn't as tall, his shoulders were broader. He had a goatee and a wicked smile. One that promised to make their morning difficult. Penelope nearly sighed. She didn't need more problems. Not when she could barely keep moving.

The hunters put their torches away, drawing swords.

Luca's sword was already in his hand. "We have

concluded our business here and plan to return home."

The wicked smile didn't falter. "Do you really think I will allow that? Humans should never enter the home of the jinni." He drew a sword, the sharp blade reflecting the light of the lantern.

Penelope froze, her gaze on the edge of the blade, her hand involuntarily going to her throat. She watched as the hunters stepped past her, Luca already in front of the guard. None of them moved, all waited for someone else to begin.

The guard chuckled. "I sense no fear from you three. Normally humans reek of it. Before I am finished, you will all know fear and tremble before the jinni in future." He leapt forward, swinging his sword at Luca.

Penelope covered her mouth with her hand, fear racing through her at how close the blade had been. Luca blocked a second attack. Malachi attacked the guard and momentarily drew his attention from Luca. It took her a few minutes to realise she should be heading for the end of the tunnel and opening the exit. It took a couple more minutes before she saw the chance to rush past them, keeping her distance from the guard. A few metres away she placed the lantern on the floor, hoping there was enough light for all of them. A pity she hadn't thought to ask one of the hunters for a torch.

After one more glance at the fight, Penelope hurried to the far end of the tunnel. It wasn't possible to go as fast as she wanted. Her body protested her demands. Reaching the far wall, she leaned against it, pressing her hand to the stone, trying to think of the words Luca had spoken. "I entered of my own free will, granted passage into the home of the jinni. I leave of my own free will, returning to the mortal world I left behind."

For a few seconds she thought nothing would happen, that she'd got the words wrong. The rock separated, sliding apart from a central point in front of her fingertips so she was forced to move her hand with the stone. The opening grew larger, the tunnel stretching out in front of her, the blackness too deep for the lantern to penetrate more than a metre. When the stone stopped moving, a large arched tunnel having formed, Penelope looked over her shoulder, keeping her hand in place.

The fight continued, the three of them staying out of the guard's reach, striking and retreating as they moved around him. No matter how quick the guard turned, the group were always out of reach, one of them attacking him from behind. Malachi grinned, both his swords moving swiftly. Alex looked serious and Luca was focused. They were all graceful and Penelope envied them their ability. She had no idea what she'd use the skill for, but she wanted to learn to fight like them. Wanted to be able to look out for herself, not stand back and leave it to others to protect her.

Pushing aside thoughts of the future, Penelope took a deep breath. "We can go."

Alex dropped back first, collecting the lantern as he went, the other two slowly retreating, drawing the jinn back with them. When he reached Penelope, Alex handed her the lantern, stepping into the tunnel. He didn't go far, only a couple of metres before he turned and faced the fight, his sword up.

"Go." Luca nodded towards Malachi, who stepped back from the fight, continuing to face it until he was well out of range, turning as he entered the tunnel.

Before Penelope could tell Luca to hurry up, the guard dashed past him, attacking her. She stumbled back, her hand coming away from the stone. The jinn swung at her again.

Luca's sword blocked the attack. "Run."

"What about you?" She backed up slowly, terrified the tunnel would close before he could escape. Already the stone was moving.

"Go. I'll be right behind you."

Wanting to protest, she turned and ran towards the hunters who'd taken out their torches and were running for the exit. She was surprised she managed to move so fast when all she wanted to do was collapse. Behind she could hear the sound of metal striking on metal. Glancing over her shoulder she saw Luca fought the guard, the tunnel slowly closing. She came to a stumbling stop, facing the fight. "Luca! Hurry up."

He glanced towards her, ducking the swinging blade. "Run."

"Not without you." The tunnel kept closing. She wanted to run to the exit. But she also wanted to run towards Luca.

"Go." After one last attack, Luca turned and ran into the tunnel, the jinn yelling at Luca to face him, calling him a coward. "Run, Penny."

She stared at him a second longer before she turned and ran, the tunnel low enough she had to duck her head slightly. Then it was lower and she was tumbling out at the other end, Alex helping her to her feet and taking the lantern from her. She faced the tunnel, her heart racing as she waited for Luca to join them. The tunnel kept closing. "Luca!"

He forced himself out of the narrow gap,

straightening as he closed the distance between them. His arms went around her. "I'm here." His grip tightened. "You're safe."

Alex rubbed at his left wrist. "Maybe not for long. There are demons in the area."

Malachi was doing the same. "I'm hoping it's more than one because if it isn't I'm not sure we'll be able to face a demon that powerful."

Penelope closed her eyes, sagging against Luca. She couldn't face anything else. Exhaustion dragged at her, making her want to sleep for a week. Even the ground looked comfortable.

Alex's phone beeped, Penelope's doing the same. He took out his phone and checked his messages. "It's Emily. They're outside watching Chad and his demons. She said they're minor ones so they can remain there day or night. She wants us to call her before we go outside."

Chapter Twenty-Four

Wondering if her message was from Emily, Penelope checked her phone, continuing to lean against Luca. Seeing it was from her mother, she began to wish she hadn't bothered checking. *How long do you plan to be out of coverage? Do you realise how inconvenient it is?* Her mother had no idea. Inconvenient wouldn't have been the word she chose. After sending a text, she returned her phone to her pocket. *I'll call you when I have better coverage.* "I'm surprised we're able to get any coverage here."

"It will be due to the entrance to the home of the jinni being recently opened. The effect will last about twelve hours," Luca said.

Alex rang Emily, putting the phone on speaker so they could all hear, letting her know the moment she answered. She told them they were on speaker too.

There was a lot of static making some of her words indistinct.

"What's happening out there?" Alex asked.

"They've set up camp in a clearing not far from the vehicle," Emily said. "Dan and I joined Scarlett, Jesse, Cassidy and Gabe as soon as we learned they were camping here waiting for you to return. I'm sorry we weren't here when you needed us."

"You had other things to deal with," Alex said. "How many demons are there?"

"Sixteen."

Malachi sat on the ground, leaning against the rock wall. "I hate to say it, but I don't think any of us are up for another fight." He slowly shook his head. "Never thought the day would come when I'd say those words."

Emily laughed softly. "None of us ever expected you to say those words."

"There's only six of us out here," Dan said. "Not enough to take on sixteen demons and Chad. He has at least three guns with him from what we could see."

"He regularly carries four," Luca said.

"We could call for reinforcements," Scarlett said. "But I don't know how long they'll take to arrive. There's been a lot of demon activity lately."

"Give us a couple of hours to rest and we'll be good to go again," Malachi said.

"Alex?" Scarlett asked. "What do you think?"

Alex smiled fleetingly. "That Malachi is overestimating his capabilities and planning to rush headlong into danger again. We'd need four or five hours. Even then we won't be at our best."

There was a moment of silence before Scarlett spoke again. "Take a break. We'll call you if anything changes."

"Okay," Alex said.

"And Alex."

"Yeah?"

"Be careful."

Alex again fleetingly smiled at his sister's words. "You too." Disconnecting the call, he sat near Malachi.

Since the hunters' torches were on, Penelope turned off the lantern Alex had left on the ground near her, returning it to Luca before she staggered over to the wall and sat down, her back against the rough stone. "This rock feels more comfortable than it should."

"Tell me about it," Malachi muttered. "Like being on a feather mattress."

"I wouldn't go that far." She leaned against Luca

when he sat next to her. "I–" Her words were interrupted by a yawn. She tried again. "I could sleep for a week."

Luca slipped his arm around her shoulders. "You'll feel better after a few hours sleep."

She knew she wouldn't, but was too tired to argue. Her eyes closed and she sank more heavily against Luca, drifting off to sleep to the sound of his heartbeat. The sound of a phone ringing woke her. She blinked, realising the torches had been turned off. She wished she'd kept the lantern.

Alex turned on his torch before answering the phone. "You're on speaker, Scarlett."

"It'll be dark out here in less than two hours. How long were you planning to sleep?"

Alex stumbled to his feet. "Did you find anyone else to help?"

"No one could get away," Gabe said. "You'd think it was Halloween with the amount of demons about."

"There are more demons at Halloween?" Groaning, Penelope staggered to her feet.

"There are more people calling on demons at Halloween," Gabe said.

"Oh." She supposed that made sense.

"We'll be out in about half an hour. We'll meet you in the clearing," Alex said.

"Don't go hogging all the fun," Malachi teased.

Cassidy laughed. "Then don't take too long to get here."

Malachi chuckled and Alex disconnected the call before Malachi could say anything else to Cassidy. "You heard her. We need to get moving."

Penelope glared at Malachi. "How can you move?" If anything, she felt worse after her sleep.

"You'll feel better once you've moved around for a bit," Malachi said.

She doubted it, but kept that comment to herself. She leaned against Luca when he slid an arm around her waist, walking slowly beside him as they headed for the mine exit.

The walk was silent and Luca unlocked the door when they reached the end of the tunnel, pushing it open to let them out, having stepped out first. His sword was drawn and he scanned the area.

Penelope stopped beside him, looking at the areas he visually searched. She could see nothing. Nor hear anything. A glance at the hunters showed they both rubbed at their wrists, sharing a look before they faced the direction of the clearing.

Luca locked the door, returning the key to his pocket. "Is everyone ready?" When they nodded, he started forward, remaining in the lead. Again they were silent, eventually stepping into the clearing.

Chad stood in the middle of the clearing along with sixteen demons. He pointed a gun at Luca. "They tell me you're human. You're no use to me anymore."

Emily and the other hunters stepped into the clearing from the other side. "You might not want to shoot him in front of so many witnesses."

"Who says there'll be any witnesses by the time the demons have finished with you?" Chad asked.

"Send the demons away. I've kept proof of some things you'll prefer the police not to look at too closely," Luca warned Chad.

"That is not part of the deal," one of the demons warned.

"You promised us whatever blood we could take from this battle," another demon said.

"The fight will not be easy for you," Luca warned the demons. "It might be best to leave while you have the chance.

Chad laughed. "You're human." He gestured towards one of the demons. "I asked them twice. Both times they said you're no longer a jinn. What do you think you can do against demons?"

"Do you think that will matter?" Luca raised his

sword. "I've trained as a warrior for centuries. Becoming human again doesn't change the past."

Cassidy drew her sword, grinning. "I love a good fight. You want my blood? Try and take it." She glanced at Gabe. "This time I plan to get up close and personal."

Gabe laughed. "Your favourite technique."

The demons attacked first, splitting into two even groups to take on the two groups of hunters coming at them. Chad fired at Luca, who ran towards the man, knocking the gun from his hands. It didn't matter. Chad had another one in his hand in seconds.

Anger rushed through Penelope. She was sick of always standing back. Being the one they protected. All the demons were occupied with hunters. She doubted she could take them on with only a dagger. But Chad was human. Remembering how the jinn had held a dagger to her throat, she tried to sneak up behind Chad. At the last second he turned to face her, the gun pointed at her face. She froze.

"Drop your sword and I won't shoot her," Chad said.

"Maybe not straight away, but he will shoot me." Penelope was surprised at how calm she sounded. Nothing at all like how she felt.

"I give you my word I won't shoot you." Chad

took a step towards her, the gun remaining pointed at her face.

"That won't stop the demons from attacking me." Penelope resisted the urge to back away. She couldn't move faster than a bullet.

"Step around where I can see you," Chad ordered Luca.

He did as he was told, standing beside Penelope, the battle continuing around them. "Killing us will not help. If I don't regularly check in, a package will be sent to the police."

"I don't believe you." Chad kept his gaze on Penelope.

"Your belief or lack of belief will not change a thing. In two days the police will receive a package with all the proof they need to incarcerate you and Eugene for the rest of your lives."

"I want proof."

"I can send you a digital copy if you let me use my phone."

"Lower your sword first."

Penelope wanted to beg Luca not to give up his weapon. Her hand tightened on the dagger she held when he placed his sword on the ground, taking out his phone. A glance around showed the hunters continued to fight the demons, there seeming to be less of the creatures now. She couldn't bring herself to take her gaze off the gun long enough to count.

Luca lowered his phone. "It's sent. Almost everything I have a hard copy of. There are a few other things I'll leave you to wonder about." His lips curved into a smile, making him look unconcerned.

Penelope hoped he wasn't bluffing. If she had to stare at the gun much longer she might do something crazy. Something even Malachi wouldn't consider doing.

Chad took out his phone and, keeping the gun trained on Penelope, checked what Luca had sent. His gun slowly lowered as he scrolled through the information, his shoulders seeming to shrink in on themselves. "I need proof you have a hard copy of this."

Penelope kept watch on the gun that was now at Chad's side.

"I'll send you a couple of pieces. That's all."

Chad nodded.

Luca took a step towards Chad. "You'll not cause problems for us. Understand?"

Again Chad nodded.

"Leave before I change my mind."

Chad glanced around at the ongoing battle. "The demons-"

"Are no longer your concern." Luca picked up his sword. "Now go."

Chad looked from one to the other. "My father won't live for much longer. A lot of this information is about him."

Luca smiled mirthlessly. "Read more carefully. You'll see more than enough references to you."

Chad glared at him before he grabbed the gun he'd dropped earlier. He stalked away, avoiding the fight.

Penelope turned to watch him go, Luca rushing past her to help Malachi with the demons he fought. She slowly turned around, having no idea what to do.

"Here." Jesse stopped beside her, offering her a handful of small vials. "Holy water to throw at them." He was gone again the moment she took the vials.

She stared at the clear liquid in the vials, not sure how they'd help. Uncapping one, she moved closer to where Luca fought a pale skinned demon, gossamer, bat-like wings stretched out behind it. She tossed the contents on the demon who roared, turning towards her.

Before the demon could go after Penelope, Luca was between them, his sword driving the creature back.

Penelope turned around, checking to see who else needed help. She smiled when she saw Cassidy and

Gabe, taking on more than their fair share of demons. They obviously didn't need any help. She spotted Alex, three demons surrounding him. Moving closer, she tossed the contents of one of the vials at a demon, stumbling backwards when he turned away from Alex and came after her.

Malachi rushed forward, attacking the demon before it could reach her. "What did you plan to do next?" He was grinning.

"I have no idea." She hadn't thought that far ahead. Hadn't expected him to go after her when Alex had been closer.

Luca joined them, driving the demon back. "The holy water will not kill them. Only cause pain and anger them. Be careful which ones you throw it on."

"I wish someone had told me that earlier," Penelope muttered.

"Throw another lot at it," Malachi ordered. "On it's chest."

She obeyed, relieved when the liquid splashed across the correct area.

Malachi drove one of his swords into the demon, forcing it back against a tree so it was unable to escape, saying words under his breath, Luca turning away to take on another demon.

"Quit it, Malachi," Gabe called out. "No praying today."

Malachi laughed, continuing his prayer, the demon vanishing in a puff of smoke after a few more words. "He was too close to going for me to stop." While he spoke, he ran towards one of the demons Scarlett fought.

Penelope stood in the middle of the chaos, clutching the vials and having no idea what to do. There were only as many demons as hunters left. Then there were less. One by one the demons vanished. Some going in a puff of smoke, others more spectacularly. Two tried to run, prevented by Cassidy and Gabe. They pleaded to be let go.

Cassidy knelt on the demon she'd pressed into the dirt. "And let you go after humans? No way." She drove her sword into the demon.

Gabe joined her, a dagger in his hand, plunging it into the creature. It became a black fog, rolling across the ground, dispersing into nothing. Gabe held out a hand to help Cassidy to her feet. Grinning, the hunter took it.

Penelope continued to stand in the middle of the clearing, unable to believe it was over. They'd beaten sixteen demons. Although she guessed she shouldn't be surprised with how they all fought. She held out the vials to Jesse when he walked towards her, Scarlett at his side.

He took them with a nod. "We'll get going if everyone is okay." He turned to Alex and Malachi. "Need a lift?"

Alex sheathed his sword, nodding before he turned to Luca. "What do you plan to do now you're human?"

Malachi grinned, sheathed his swords and clapped Luca on the back. "You can fight at my side any time." He grinned. "Or help out with clean up."

"I am going home. After that..." Luca shrugged. "I don't know. I've spent my entire life in one battle or another. It's the only way of life I've known."

Alex held out a hand, shaking Luca's. "Give me a call if you're interested. There are always plenty of demons to be fought." He scribbled his number on the back of a business card and gave it to Luca.

Chapter Twenty-Five

The hunters left after they'd said goodbye, the sound of their engines fading into the distance. Luca took out the lantern, turning it on for the walk back to his vehicle. They were silent.

Penelope sat in the passenger seat, trying to think of a way to ask him what he planned to do next. In the end she drifted off to sleep, waking when the engine was silent. Blinking, it took her a few seconds to realise she was at Luca's house.

He opened the driver's door, looking at her before he got out. "I thought you might want to see Rusty."

"Yes." She'd begun to hope he'd brought her here for another reason. Like not wanting to part with her.

Half out of the vehicle, Luca turned to look at her again. "What is wrong?"

"I'm tired."

"Go see Rusty and have a shower while I make us something to eat."

She reached for him, resting her hand on his arm. "You need sleep too."

"I know." He stared at her a moment longer before he got out of the vehicle.

She walked inside with him, leaving him in the kitchen when she headed out the back to check on Rusty, grinning at the dog's enthusiastic greeting. Burying her face in his fur, she was surprised by the tears that coursed down her face. She should be happy. The curse was broken and they'd survived. She stayed outside with Rusty until Luca called her in to dinner, drying her eyes before she went inside.

Not knowing what to say, Penelope again remained silent. When she would have left the table after she'd eaten, Luca took her hand. She stared at her hand covered by his, eventually meeting his gaze when he didn't speak.

"What is wrong?"

She thought of and discarded numerous comments. "I don't want to go home." She didn't want to leave him.

"You're welcome to stay as long as you wish. Or I could buy you your own place."

"That wouldn't be right. I can't take your money."

Rising, Luca came around the table to stand beside her, drawing her to her feet. "I owe you my life. My human life. A house is nothing in comparison. Have you forgotten I have more money than I can spend in a single lifetime?" His lips slowly curved into a smile. "That's all I have left. A single lifetime."

It wasn't his house or his money that she wanted. Her courage momentarily failed her. Reminding herself she'd faced giant creatures, jinni and demons, she took a deep breath. "I don't want you to leave."

Luca frowned, continuing to hold her hand. "You do not want me to go home?"

She shook her head. "I don't want you to leave me."

Luca grinned, engulfing her in his embrace, his lips meeting hers. They remained entwined for long minutes, both eventually drawing away at the same time. Luca's grin returned. "Never."

Penelope yawned, having tried to stop it.

"Sleep. We'll talk in the morning."

She wanted to protest, but found herself yawning again. Before she headed to bed, she showered and then checked on Rusty once more, smiling when she found him sleeping in front of the back door. His eyes opened and his tail thumped on the patio floor when he saw her.

Sleep came instantly and was dreamless. She woke

feeling rested, her body aching from all the exercise of the past couple of days, Luca's arms wrapped around her. Stretching, she smiled in greeting when her movements woke him. "I need to go home. Can Rusty stay here?"

Luca played with a strand of her hair. "Both of you can."

She liked the sound of his words. "I need to sort through some things first." She didn't want to move in with him as a way to escape her family. She needed to make sure she was moving in for the right reasons. "How about we meet up for lunch?"

They decided on a venue and after breakfast, and spending some time with Rusty, Penelope drove home. Her good mood evaporated when she reached her room. The smell of fresh paint was faint, but as obvious as the new colours on the walls. Her hand tightened into a fist and she thought of the dagger she'd left at Luca's place. A house that had felt more like home than this one ever had.

Her anger faded. Home. It wasn't here and it wasn't Luca's house. It was him. A sound had her spinning to see the housekeeper walking towards her.

"There's a box of items in the back of your walk-in wardrobe I packed up for you."

She guessed the housekeeper meant Luca's clothes. "Thank you. But it didn't matter."

"You never would have heard the end of it."

She smiled, shrugging. "That doesn't matter anymore."

"Your mother asked to be informed when you arrived."

Penelope glanced up the hallway, half expecting to see her mother. "Give me a quarter of an hour."

"If I can."

After the housekeeper strode away, Penelope entered the bedroom, taking the box to her car first. Returning to her room, she took out a suitcase and began to fill it with her favourite clothes. It was only half full, the contents of the walk-in wardrobe barely touched.

"What are you doing?"

Penelope turned to see her mother in the doorway. "Moving out."

"That is an inappropriate reaction to having your room redecorated. "

Anger rushed back in on her. She was glad she'd already figured out she wasn't running from anything, but running to Luca. This moment would have had her worried about her motives. "That's not what I'm annoyed about. Did you ask if I wanted my room changed?"

"It needed updating. The scheme was looking old and worn."

"After five months? That's your opinion. What about mine?"

"Surely you didn't want to remain in such inappropriate surroundings."

Penelope's gaze travelled over her mother, taking in every perfect inch of her from her styled hair to her new dress. "I like worn out jeans that are so comfortable they feel like a second skin."

"What does that have to do with the colour scheme of your room?"

She thought of Luca's eyes. "And I love the colour blue. A bright, intense, dark blue."

"Next time that colour can be incorporated into the scheme."

"I hate having my room changed every year. Sometimes twice a year. Just like I hate getting rid of my jeans once they're properly worn in."

"You're not making any sense."

Penelope smiled, thinking of Suzie and Harrison. The supposedly appropriate friend and boyfriend. "Actually, I am. The only problem is, it doesn't make sense to you." She turned away, zipping up her suitcase.

"You have nowhere to go."

Lifting the surprisingly light suitcase, she faced her mother. "Actually, I do." She smiled, knowing how Luca had felt when he'd said it. "I'm going home." She moved towards her mother, not surprised that she stepped out of the way. She strode along the hallway without bothering to look back. Reaching her car, she checked the time. It was too early to meet Luca. She'd go shopping and buy herself some inappropriate clothes. Ones that were appropriate for her. Ones she'd be able to train in.

It didn't take her long to buy clothes and she decided to take everything back to Luca's house. There was more than enough time. Then they could go to lunch together. But he wasn't home. Only Rusty was. She patted the dog. "Want to come to lunch with us." His enthusiasm made her laugh. "Okay. Let's go."

She put him on the back seat, having already taken everything inside, and headed towards the cafe. Rusty would be able to join them at the outside tables where people often ate with their dog's lead tied to their chair. Arriving, she found an empty table and was about to sit when Suzie came towards her.

"I haven't seen you about for days. Where have you been?"

"I've been busy." Fighting demons and breaking a curse. A look of shock crossed Suzie's face and for a moment Penelope feared she'd spoken the words aloud.

"Don't tell me that ugly thing is yours." Suzie pointed to Rusty, taking a step back as if he was a contagious disease.

Penelope stared at Suzie, trying to put all her effort into looking amazed. "You mean to say you'd buy a designer dog when there are so many abandoned and abused dogs in desperate need of a home?"

"Of course not. I..." Suzie trailed off glancing around.

Penelope almost smiled. If her habit was twisting her hair between her fingers when she was uncomfortable, Suzie's was looking around as if trying to find a way to escape. "Are you sure? I could have sworn that's what you meant."

"Of course it wasn't." Suzie checked the time on her phone. "I have to go. I've got things to do." She smiled insincerely.

Penelope gave her the same fake smile. "Of course." Her smile widened when Suzie's faded. She continued to grin as she watched her ex-friend hurry away.

Rusty pressed a damp nose against her hand.

She patted his head. "Suzie was wrong, you know. You're the most beautiful dog in the world." A chuckle behind her had her turning to face Luca. "Do you disagree?"

He grinned. "I wouldn't dare after how fast I saw Suzie leave the area." His grin faded. "I tried to get here quicker, but I'm not as fast as I once was."

"That's okay. I had it all under control. You don't need to protect me from everything."

"I know. But it's my pleasure to look out for you."

She didn't know if she should be annoyed. "What if I want to look out for you?"

"I'd feel honoured."

"You would?"

He nodded, smiling as he drew something from a pocket. "I have a gift for you."

She stared at the plane ticket he held out. "You're going?"

He continued to smile. "Take it."

She reluctantly took the ticket, realising there were two of them. Her gaze was drawn to Luca and she struggled to think of what to say. Words seemed to have fled, leaving her speechless.

Luca's smile faded. "Do you not want to go home with me?" His accent was heavier than usual.

She threw her arms around him, her lips meeting his. Eventually she drew back, grinning. "I'd love to go home with you."

"I want you there when I collect my sword."

"You can't do that. How will you explain why you know where it is?"

"I have a letter I wrote centuries ago bequeathing it to my descendents and describing the location. I've always made certain the letter was kept in a safe place."

"How will you prove you're a descendent?"

"Do you think they will doubt who I am when there are paintings of me hanging in the castle?"

Penelope chuckled. "They'll think you're a ghost."

Luca grinned. "If only they knew the truth."

She laughed, tightening her arms around him. "Yeah, if only." She kissed him again, glad for the curse that had allowed her to meet him, but happier it had finally been broken. She drew back to meet his gaze. "Are you excited you're going home?"

"I'm excited I will again see my family home, but you're wrong. I'm not going home. I'm already there."

She held his gaze, thinking for a moment that she

felt his emotions. Or maybe they were her own. It didn't matter who they belonged to. She tightened her arms around him. "I know. It's good to be home." His lips met hers and she clung to him, not caring who watched them or what they thought. She planned for life to be a lot more inappropriate in the future. At least according to her family. But what would they know? They'd never faced demons, travelled to the home of the jinni or broken a curse. She'd done all three and would do a lot more in the future. Both her and Luca.

Chapter Twenty-Six

Penelope threw the ball for Rusty, remaining in the shade on the patio, grinning as she watched him run enthusiastically after it. They'd been back from Italy for two weeks now. The nearly three months they'd spent there had been some of the best and craziest moments of her life. The emails she'd initially received from her mother had been full of negative comments about going overseas with someone she didn't know and the dangers of doing so. The tone of the emails had changed when newspapers began to display headlines like 'Lost Conte Claims His Title And The Sword Of His Ancestor'. Luca now had both his sword and his father's, the other two swords remaining with the rest of his relatives.

Rusty dropped the ball at her feet, sitting in front of her, his tail brushing back and forth rapidly. She threw the ball again, her gaze scanning the backyard, so different from the castle they'd stayed at. Luca's family had insisted they stay with them, continually marvelling over how much he looked like his ancestor. Each time they'd said so, she'd been tempted to laugh.

Hearing the backdoor open, she turned to see Luca step outside. She smiled at the sight of him in his black jeans and button up shirt, his hair damp from a recent shower. Even casual clothes looked formal on him.

Luca held out her phone. "You left it on the kitchen bench. We're on clean up duty this week."

"I heard a noise and thought I should check on it." She took the phone from him, sliding it into a pocket of her jeans before wrapping her arms around him.

He held her close. "Was there something that needed your attention?" He smiled. "Other than Rusty?"

The dog barked once at hearing his name, the ball dropping from his mouth so he had to pick it up again.

Penelope grinned. "He was lonely. And you weren't here."

"You didn't want to come to the gym."

"I'll go with you tonight, after training." She was surprised at how quickly she was progressing in learning how to fight with both a sword and a bow. Luca was a good teacher. His family in Italy had commented on his skill, having sometimes watched as he taught her the correct way to handle and use the weapons. They'd continued training when they returned home. So far she'd been in a single fight, having used the bow as she joined Malachi and Alex when they faced two demons. Between the four of them the demons hadn't lasted long.

Luca lightly brushed his lips across hers. "You're happy?" He paused a moment. "With everything?"

"Yes. I was thinking about it before you came out." It was uncanny how often he seemed to almost read her thoughts. Neither of them should be able to sense each other's emotions and yet at times it seemed they did. "The past months have been some of the best and craziest moments of my life." Her arms tightened around him. "I wouldn't change a thing."

Rusty pawed at Penelope's leg, the ball on the patio floor, his eyes begging for it to be thrown again.

Penelope held onto Luca with one arm, reaching out to rub Rusty's head. "Sorry, boy. Was I ignoring you?" Before she could throw the ball again, her phone rang. Checking the display, she saw it was from Malachi. Excitement raced through her. "Hello. You're on speaker."

"Is it safe to talk?"

Penelope watched as Luca threw the ball for Rusty. "Unless it's something Rusty shouldn't hear."

Malachi chuckled. "How do you feel about trespassing? Father Joe received a call about two creatures appearing out of nowhere and walking in the front door of a house in a suburb not far from our two places."

Penelope had been surprised to learn Malachi lived only five minutes from them. She looked to Luca, who nodded. "Sounds good. What should we bring?"

"Swords. It'll be too close quarters for bows. Can you be there in about twenty? Or did you want me to pick you up?"

"Send us the address. We'll meet you there," Luca said.

"Will do. See you soon." Malachi disconnected, a text message coming through a minute later.

Penelope stared at the address, heart racing. This time it wasn't with fear. She was finally going to have the chance to fight demons with a sword. She glanced towards the backyard where she'd spent many hours training since they'd returned. Sometimes various hunters had joined them, Luca often sharing his centuries of experience with them.

Luca took her hand. "Are you certain this is what you want to do?"

She slipped the phone in her pocket. "Cassidy said she'd teach me how to use ninja stars." The hunter had asked her why Luca sometimes called her 'little ninja'. "Shurikens."

Luca inclined his head. "I'll collect our weapons. You lock the house."

It didn't take long to gather their gear and drive to the address Malachi had given them. They parked behind his car, which he leaned against. Pushing away from his car, Malachi strode towards them, his swords at his sides.

Penelope scanned the area as she got out of the four-wheel-drive, rubbing her hand across the small black mark on the inside of her wrist that she'd gained in her previous fight. "I can feel demons in the area."

Malachi grinned. "You'll get used to it."

"I hope not. It's an amazing feeling to know we can sense them even when they try to hide themselves from the rest of the world."

Luca took their swords out of the back of the vehicle. "These ones obviously didn't care if anyone saw them." His gaze scanned the quiet street, numerous old trees creating shadowy areas along the footpath. "Not that there seems to be anyone about."

Penelope took her sword, strapping it on. "I hope not. We don't want the next call to be to the police."

Malachi laughed. "They're likely to be put through to Detective Tuck. He always gets the strange calls." He looked from one to the other. "Ready to see what these demons are up to?"

Penelope glanced at Luca, nodding her head when he inclined his. She faced Malachi again. "Lead the way."

"Preferably not straight into trouble," Luca said dryly.

Malachi laughed. "About the only thing I can promise is it'll be fun."

Penelope walked at Malachi's side, dropping back when he entered an open gate. She didn't doubt he was unable to promise not to lead them into trouble. Not after some of the stories she'd heard since returning to Brisbane. She stared at the sprawling timber house in front of her. It was old, but well maintained. Not the sort of place where most people would expect to find demons. She knew better. They could be found anywhere except sacred ground.

Luca followed Penelope through the gate, stopping at her side the moment they were in the front yard. Three large trees with widespread branches hid most of the house from the street. He looked over his shoulder before scanning the rest of the yard. "It would have been the neighbour across the street who called. That's the only one with a clear view of the front door."

Malachi looked towards the street, nodding after he finished checking out the area. "I'll go in the back if you two want to go in the front. Give me five minutes."

Luca drew his sword. "Text us if you need longer."

Malachi drew one of his swords before striding around the side of the house.

Penelope watched him go before glancing over her shoulder. "Do you think the neighbour will ring the police?"

"I have a feeling the neighbour will ring Father Joe first. To see if he sent us."

"I hope so."

"What is wrong?"

She nearly said nothing, smiling instead. "Old habits are hard to break." She shrugged. "If we end up in jail at least it'd give my family something to actually complain about." A grin escaped. "But I bet they would continue to fawn over you. They'd probably say it was me leading you astray."

Luca checked the time on the watch that had once held his medallion. He'd told her it was a reminder of what they'd achieved. His freedom. Luca's gaze met hers. "Lead the way. I'd follow you anywhere. Even into trouble."

She faced the house, scanning the place for signs of movement. There were none. She cautiously headed for the front door, surprised to find it was unlocked. The demons were inside somewhere. Minor demons. But they would be no less dangerous for being minor ones. Stepping inside the dim interior, she listened. The house was silent.

Luca shut the door behind them. "They're towards the back left corner of the house. Do you want me to go ahead?"

"No. I've got this." She wasn't about to stand back and let others protect her. She'd done more than enough of that. Keeping her sword up, she continued through the house, meeting up with Malachi in a hallway. Before she could say anything to him, a scream rang out through the house.

"That came from the back left corner," Luca said.

"Sounds like demons causing trouble to me." Malachi ran along the hallway.

Penelope chased after him, hearing Luca's footsteps behind her. They burst into a bedroom, spreading out as they entered the door. Two demons were in front of them, one holding a young woman who appeared to be around her age.

The demons faced them, one grinning as he formed a sword from the air. "No one said the day would be so interesting. Four humans to play with."

"I don't think the day's going to be much fun for you." Malachi drew his second sword, racing towards the demon that held the terrified young woman.

With a glance at Luca, Penelope attacked the second demon. Weeks of training made the action feel familiar. Her sword connected with that of the demon. She couldn't have fought the creature on her own, but she held her ground, meeting the blade each time it came for her.

The demon was quicker than her and Luca and it took both of them to fight it. Worried Malachi might need help, she fought harder, needing to send the creature back to hell.

"You waste your time," the demon said. "No sooner do one of you hunters return us to hell than some stupid human is summoning us." He grinned, rows of pointed teeth crowding his mouth. "You can never get rid of us permanently."

Luca blocked the demon's sword. "We'll return you to hell as often as necessary."

Seeing an opening, Penelope drove her sword into

the demon, satisfaction rushing through her at his howl of pain. "Some can never return to our world." She'd pestered the hunters to tell her everything about demons, reading some of the many books they had on the subject. "One day you'll be barred from this world too."

The demon launched himself at her, his sword vanishing as claws were aimed at her face. "Never. I'll always return and one day you'll be dead and no longer able to stop me."

Penelope threw herself to the side. When Luca attacked the demon and caused it to turn on him, she continued attacking. "It doesn't matter. There will always be others to take our place." Generations of hunters had protected humans and generations more would continue to do so. Again she attacked, cutting the demon's arm, dark blood instantly staining his motley coloured flesh. "It is demons that are stupid, thinking they can ever win." She drove the demon back towards the wall, pinning him there with Luca's help. She liked being part of the hunters, a family she could be proud of. They might not be related to any of them, but they'd welcomed her and Luca as one of their own.

Luca drew a dagger, plunging it into the demon. "Return to where you came from."

Smoke rose from the wound and the demon shrieked, trying to escape.

Penelope kept the demon pinned, struggling to hold him, even with Luca's help. "You aren't welcome in this world. No matter how many summon you there'll always be those of us who send you back." Just when she thought he might escape, the smoke rising from around the dagger, that had been dipped in holy water, enveloped his entire body and she found herself stumbling against the wall, the demon gone.

Luca looked her up and down. "You're unhurt?"

She nodded, pushing away from the wall. "Malachi needs our help." It was good not to be the one needing help for a change.

Luca inclined his head, joining her as she attacked the other demon.

It didn't take long to return the demon to hell. He went in a burst of light, causing all of them to shield their eyes. The three of them faced the young woman who'd retreated to a corner of the room, her eyes wide.

Penelope stood with her sword in her hand, heart still racing. She had no idea what to do next. No one had explained this part to her. Only how to deal with demons.

Malachi sheathed his swords, taking a couple of steps towards the young woman. "Are you okay?"

The young woman nodded, then shook her head. "How-" She looked at each of them. "I've never-" Again she stopped abruptly.

Malachi stepped a little closer. "You're safe now."

The young woman shook her head, fumbling in her handbag to draw out a tissue. She pressed it against a deep scratch at her wrist. "How can any of this be real?" She looked from them to the wound, an occasional glance around the room.

Penelope knew exactly how she felt. Shocked, confused and afraid.

"Why were they after you?" Luca asked.

"I'm nobody." The young woman checked her wrist. "Nobody." Blood welled up along the scratch and she pressed the tissue against it again. Her gaze met Penelope's. "Why are you here? Why did you help me?"

Penelope stared at the young woman. It seemed like forever since she'd been in the same position. Frightened and having no idea what to do. Her heart continued to race, but it wasn't from fear. A smile formed. "We're hunters. This is our job. It's what we do."

Malachi closed the distance between him and the

young woman, putting an arm around her shoulders. "Let me take you home." He glanced at Luca.

"We'll take care of things here."

Penelope watched Malachi lead the dazed young woman from the room, sheathing her sword when she realised she continued to hold it. A glance around the room showed there was a lot of cleaning up to do. "Why doesn't it surprise me that Malachi got the easier job?" Her smile didn't falter.

Luca chuckled. "You don't mind?"

She shook her head. The words she'd said to the young woman returned to her. She stepped closer, wrapping her arms around him, her gaze meeting his when he slid his arms around her. "We're hunters. This is our job." And she loved every minute of it. Her smile became a grin as she thought of what her grandmother would say. Her grandmother had no idea. This was the appropriate life for her, not the one her family wanted.

Free Ebook

Subscribe to Avril's newsletter to receive a free ebook. This ebook is exclusive to those on her mailing list. To find out more about this offer visit: www.avrilsabine.com/free-ebook

*

We value your privacy and will not sell, rent, exchange or loan your email address to third parties. Your information is confidential and you are under no obligation to remain on the mailing list and can unsubscribe at any time.

Acknowledgements

Thank you to the usual crew. As always, your help is invaluable.

To The Reader

If you enjoyed this book, why not consider leaving a review to help other readers discover it too? Reader engagement is one of the few ways that lets an author know readers want more books in a particular series or genre. So leave a review and tell friends, not only about this book but also about other ones you've enjoyed, so you can continue to enjoy books by your favourite authors for years to come.

Dreams are meant to be lived,

Avril.

About The Author

Avril is an Australian author who lives with her family on acreage in South East Queensland. She writes mostly young adult speculative fiction, but has been known to dabble in other genres. You can find more information about her at her website www.avrilsabine.com where you can also subscribe to her newsletter to be kept informed about new releases, current projects, blog posts and exclusive news.

Titles By Avril Sabine

Stories about strong characters and characters who discover their strengths.

SERIES

Assassins Of The Dead- Young Adult Fantasy/ Paranormal

Book 1: Dark Blade

Book 2: Dragon Touched

Book 3: Society Against Vampires

Book 4: King's Request

Dragon Blood- Young Adult Urban Fantasy (with elements of romance)

(5 book series)

Book 1: Pliethin

Book 2: Wyvern

Book 3: Surety

Book 4: Knight

Book 5: Mage

Dragon Mage- Young Adult Urban Fantasy (with elements of romance)

(Series two of Dragon Blood series)

Book 1: Promise

Dragon Blood Chronicles- Young Adult Urban Fantasy (with elements of romance)

(Companion stand alone series to Dragon Blood)

Book 1: Oath

Book 2: Betrayed

Guardians Of The Round Table- Young Adult Fantasy LitRPG

(Co-written with Storm and Rhys Petersen)

Book 1: Dexterity Fail

Book 2: Goblin Boots

Book 3: Singed Feathers

Book 4: Frog Mage

Book 5: Crystal Mine

Book 6: Cursed Harp

Rosie's Rangers- Young Adult Western Steampunk

(6 book series)

Book 1: Justice

Book 2: Vengeance

Book 3: Treachery

Book 4: Accused

Book 5: Wanted

Book 6: Corruption

Mark Of Kings- Children's Fantasy

(Upper middle grade/preteen)

(4 book series)

Book 1: The Arena

Book 2: The Island

Book 3: The Assassin

Book 4: The King

STAND ALONE SERIES

*Demon Hunters- Young Adult Urban Fantasy/
Horror (with elements of romance)*

Book 1: Blood Sacrifice

Book 2: Retribution

Book 3: Tainted

Book 4: Premonition

Book 5: Cursed

Book 6: Feud

Book 7: Extrication

Plea Of The Damned- Young Adult Urban Fantasy/Paranormal

(6 book series)

Book 1: Forgive Me Lucy

Book 2: Forgive Me Aiden

Book 3: Forgive Me Jena

Book 4: Forgive Me Kobe

Book 5: Forgive Me Marti

Book 6: Forgive Me Dawson

Realms Of The Fae- Young Adult Urban Fantasy (with elements of romance)

The Sword (short story in Like A Girl Anthology)

Heart Of Stone

Book 1: A Debt Owed

Book 2: Marked By The Hunt

Book 3: The Magic Collector

Book 4: An Unexpected Betrayal

Book 5: Imprisoned By Iron

Fairytales Retold (Short Stories)

Snow-White And Rose-Red

The Twelve Brothers

The Light Princess

Beauty And The Beast

Sleeping Beauty

Aschenputtel

The Golden Bird

The Frog Prince

The Death Of Koshchei The Deathless

Myths And Legends Retold (Short Stories)

Ion, Son Of Apollo

Sir Gawain And The Maid With The Narrow Sleeves

Princess Ilse, The Giant's Daughter

YOUNG ADULT NOVELS

Young Adult Fantasy (with elements of romance)

Elf Sight

Earth Bound

Young Adult Urban Fantasy

Stone Warrior (with elements of romance)

The Jungle Inside

Young Adult Contemporary (with elements of romance)

Through Your Eyes

The Ugly Stepsister

Perfect Little Princess

Young Adult Contemporary/Paranormal

Whispers In The Dark (with elements of romance and same sex relationships)

Over Too Soon (with elements of romance)

Young Adult Sci-Fi

Experiment X-One-Six (Urban Sci-Fi/Superheroes)

An Endless Dawn (Post Apocalyptic Sci-Fi)

CHILDREN'S BOOKS

Dragon Lord (Preteen/early teens) (Fantasy)

The Irish Wizard (Upper middle grade) (Urban Fantasy)

SHORT STORIES

Urban Fantasy

Eternally Late

Dealings With Joe

Glimpses (short story in That Moment When
Anthology)

Contemporary

The Brat Next Door

Fantasy LitRPG

(Set in the same world as Guardians Of The Round
Table Series)

Tales Of Inadon 1: The Disc (Co-written with
Storm and Rhys Petersen) (short story in Game On!
Anthology)

Post Apocalyptic Sci-Fi

Compulsive Directive

NONFICTION

A Year Of Weekly Writing Exercises (Creative Writing)

Cooking For Families With Allergies (Cooking) (Co-written with Storm Petersen)

Tell Me A Story, Grandma (Memoir)

For the most up to date details on available titles visit:

www.avrilsabine.com/books/bibliography

Demon Hunter Series

To learn more about this series visit:

www.avrilsabine.com/series/dh

BOOKS AVAILABLE IN THE DEMON HUNTER SERIES

Book 1: Blood Sacrifice

Book 2: Retribution

Book 3: Tainted

Book 4: Premonition

Book 5: Cursed

Book 6: Feud

Book 7: Extrication

Disclaimer

This is a work of fiction. Names, characters, businesses, places, events and incidents are either the products of the author's imagination or used in a fictitious manner. Any resemblance to actual persons, living or dead, or actual events is purely coincidental. The opinions expressed or beliefs held are those of the characters and should not be assumed to be the opinions or beliefs of the author.